Maverick  barking, s_____ had caught the dog's attention.

Maverick looked in the direction Wolf was facing.

A figure skulked in the forest as red flashed through the trees, followed by another.

The gunman was back with reinforcements.

And he, Violet and Wolf were perilously close to the cliff's edge. With nowhere to run.

"Get behind the rocks!"

Violet ducked behind the skeletal grave they had unearthed.

Maverick followed and pointed to Violet. "Wolf, protect!"

The dog positioned himself beside Violet in a tight formation, his gaze still directed toward the forest.

Two masked men wearing Santa hats emerged at the tree line. One lifted a bullhorn. "We only want the archaeologist. Hand her over, and we'll let you go."

A scream lodged in Violet's throat as her heart rate escalated. Maverick wrapped a protective arm around her waist.

"You're outnumbered, Constable. Give her up." The other Santa man lifted his weapon. "Don't think that dog will save you this time. He makes one move and I shoot him..."

Darlene L. Turner is an award-winning author who lives with her husband, Jeff, in Ontario, Canada. Her love of suspense began when she read her first Nancy Drew book. She's turned that passion into her writing and believes readers will be captured by her plots, inspired by her strong characters and moved by her inspirational message. Visit Darlene at www.darlenelturner.com, where there's suspense beyond borders.

Books by Darlene L. Turner

Love Inspired Suspense

National Park Protectors

Danger in the Wilderness
Trail of Mountain Secrets

Crisis Rescue Team

Fatal Forensic Investigation
Explosive Christmas Showdown
Mountain Abduction Rescue
Buried Grave Secrets
Yukon Wilderness Evidence
K-9 Ranch Protection

Love Inspired Trade

Echoes of Darkness

Visit the Author Profile page at LoveInspired.com for more titles.

TRAIL OF MOUNTAIN SECRETS

DARLENE L. TURNER

If you purchased this book without a cover you should be aware that this book is stolen property. It was reported as "unsold and destroyed" to the publisher, and neither the author nor the publisher has received any payment for this "stripped book."

ISBN-13: 978-1-335-95742-9

Trail of Mountain Secrets

Copyright © 2025 by Darlene L. Turner

All rights reserved. No part of this book may be used or reproduced in any manner whatsoever without written permission.

Without limiting the author's and publisher's exclusive rights, any unauthorized use of this publication to train generative artificial intelligence (AI) technologies is expressly prohibited.

This is a work of fiction. Names, characters, places and incidents are either the product of the author's imagination or are used fictitiously. Any resemblance to actual persons, living or dead, businesses, companies, events or locales is entirely coincidental.

For questions and comments about the quality of this book, please contact us at CustomerService@Harlequin.com.

® is a trademark of Harlequin Enterprises ULC.

Love Inspired
22 Adelaide St. West, 41st Floor
Toronto, Ontario M5H 4E3, Canada
www.LoveInspired.com

Printed in Lithuania

The Lord is my shepherd; I shall not want.
—*Psalm* 23:1

For my sister, Sue

We're almost like twins :-)

I love you

Acknowledgments

Jeff, thank you for always being there for me and listening to my interesting story ideas. You are a treasure from God and I love you more each day.

Sue, we should have been born twins, as we sure have that same intuition. I love you to the moon and back.

Tina James, thank you for believing in my stories and helping them to shine! I appreciate you.

Tamela Hancock Murray, thank you for your continued support and direction in my writing career. You're amazing!

Fab Four and Suspense Squad, thank you for always being available to brainstorm, help me find the right word and talk me off the ledge. LOL.

Jesus, thank You for directing my path.
May I always give You the honor and glory.

ONE

Searching for a skull in the dangerous northern tip of Asterbine National Park wasn't where park archeologist Violet Hoyt wanted to be six days before Christmas, but her leader had tasked her to find the other Hancock family member who'd been missing for two years. Violet's team had discovered three other skulls in early November while searching for artifacts where historians believed a trading post had once flourished in the park. The medical examiner had identified the skulls through dental records as three members of the Hancock family—mother, father and teenage son—all shot in the head, execution style. Someone had buried the heads in the middle of Violet's excavation site. Not something she had expected to discover.

Violet adjusted her coat's zipper to block out not only the approaching storm, but the foreboding creeping through every muscle in her body. Where was her colleague? She needed to get started before the weather turned nasty. After receiving a call at seven this morning from her leader with a tip from an inmate stating eight-year-old Amy Hancock's skull was a few kilometers north of where they'd found the others, Violet had gathered her tools and headed to the park. She'd called Jill en route, but that was thirty minutes ago. She couldn't wait any longer.

A branch snapped to her right.

Violet froze and pivoted, searching the area.

Crack!

She reached into the trailer hitched to the back of her ATV and grabbed her pickax. "Who's there?"

She scanned the region, but nothing materialized. Violet expelled the breath she'd been holding. "You're paranoid. This park is safe." She chuckled. "And now you're talking to yourself." *Get a grip.* She'd been on edge ever since the media had thrust her into the spotlight after she'd discovered the skulls. She hated the attention.

Violet puffed out a breath, the vapors lingering in the frigid air, and texted her colleague Jill Mann, asking her whereabouts. She'd probably lose her signal once she ascended the steep path to where she had to begin her search. Violet tapped in her location and stated she was heading into the forest. After all, she'd been in this park by herself many times.

Her cell phone buzzed with a text.

I know who you really are. Let this family rest and stay out of the park. Or else.

She sucked in a breath. What in the world? Not Jill. Maybe she should wait for her colleague. Another ding. Her pulse revved up as she read her screen.

Have a family emergency. Should be there in an hour. Sorry. J

Ugh! Not good. Violet keyed in a reply, praying for Jill's family at the same time. She swiped back to the first message and examined the text's information. *No Caller ID.* She hit the block button to be on the safe side and stuffed her cell into her winter jacket.

Violet cleared the light dusting of snow off the yellow tape marking their original dig and studied the sky. *Keep your eyes to the skies and ears in nature.*

Her father's saying popped into her mind. Frank Hoyt had made his children repeat his mantra until they all memorized it. *Dad, you're always right about nature.*

Dark clouds were rolling in quickly along with a cool breeze, proof that the meteorologists were correct. Snow would soon hamper the region right in time for the Christmas season, which, of course, made Violet happy. She loved snow at Christmas.

A brisk wind whipped through the trees, snaking down her neck and adding to her already anxious mood. *You can do this.* She rolled her shoulders in determination, gathered her tools and backpack before heading toward the Hawkweed Mountain trail.

Forty-five minutes later, Violet unhooked her portable, ground-penetrating radar machine. Her team and police had searched all around where they found the skulls for the rest of the remains, but failed to find anything. They'd concluded that whoever killed the Hancock family had disposed the rest of their bodies elsewhere. Why, they didn't know.

"Come on, Gus. I want to finish this and get out of the forest. I have Christmas gifts to buy." Violet had nicknamed the device after Gustave, her favorite park custodian, who passed two years ago.

She waved the machine over the rocky terrain inch by inch, but nothing alerted her to skeletal remains. After another fifteen minutes of searching, she shut off the machine at the same time her sat phone rang. She jumped. Why suddenly was she scared to be in the forest by herself? Obviously, the knowledge that another Hancock family member may have been brutally murdered and buried there frayed her nerves.

Violet fished the phone out of her backpack. "Violet Hoyt here."

"Anything yet, Hoyt?" her boss, Kevin McGregor, asked.

The older gentleman had taken Violet under his wing when she got the job, but his voice, usually calm, held concern, and she knew why. The mayor was breathing down his neck ever since their skull discovery.

"Nothing. Are we sure we trust this inmate's word, sir?"

"We have no choice. The police have no other leads and deemed this a cold case. Wanted to give you a heads-up. Mayor Coble has brought in a human remains detection dog to help your team. Apparently, the dog specializes in archaeology finds.

Constable Sara Daley is escorting them to your location. They should be there soon."

"Thanks for the update." Great. Another member to add to their team and risk contaminating the site. Not that she minded. She wanted to give the rest of the Hancock family closure. Two years had been too long to wait.

"Do me proud, Violet. There's a lot riding on this case."

He didn't have to tell her twice. The press had been following the story, picking it apart with a fine-tooth comb.

And ridiculing Violet every step of the way.

"Understood, sir. I'll report our progress to you later."

"One more thing. Be careful. The inmate told the guard his cellmate has more information, so Constable Everett is at the prison questioning him. All we can ascertain at this point is it has something to do with you and the dig. It's another reason I requested police protection for you."

Violet's jaw dropped as the earlier text entered her mind. Had it been meant for her, after all? Good thing her constable friend Sara was on her way. "How would this inmate possibly know that?"

"No idea. Just had to warn you. Stay alert."

"Yes, sir. Tell Sara I'm at Hawkweed Junction. Talk later." She clicked off the call, stowed the phone in her pack's side pocket and picked up Gus. She must continue her search and vacate the forest.

After another thirty minutes of futile searching, Violet set her GPR device aside and removed her water bottle from her backpack. *Jill, where are you?*

Movement rustled the bushes behind her, and she pivoted, dropping her bottle.

A figure emerged from the shadows, dressed in camouflage gear and a white ski mask, beard and a Santa hat. He raised a rifle at her. "You can't fool me, Violet Hoyt. I know who you really are, Baylee Peck." The man's lips curved into a sneer through his mask's mouthpiece. "Where is it? I know you have it."

Violet gasped and raised her hands. "What are you talking about?"

"The evidence you compiled against me." He paused. "And now Ragnovica is out for my head, which means you're on their radar, too. You should have left those skulls in the forest. It's only a matter of time before you're dead."

Violet trembled at the man's warning. Ragnovica? Who in the world was that?

He waved the rifle at her and moved closer. "Give it to me. Now."

"I have no idea what you're talking about."

A dog barked in the distance, followed by muffled voices.

She turned at the sound. "Help!"

Santa Man yanked her into a tight hold. "No one can save you, Baylee. Not from me."

His breath reeked with the pungent smell of stale cigarette smoke and whiskey.

Violet's stomach lurched, her breakfast contents threatening to expel. *Please help me!* Her silent plea thundered in her mind.

The dog's bark increased, and she glanced at the trail as the man tightened his grip. Spots prickled her vision, like fireflies, and her world spun. *Fight it, Violet. Breathe.*

A man and a dog appeared in her foggy line of sight. She recognized the blond from her past. Someone she had hoped never to see again, but was now thankful for his presence.

Maverick?

Santa Man raised his rifle. "Stop or she dies."

Terror overpowered Violet, and her knees buckled. *Lord, save me!*

K-9 handler Maverick Shaw caught the woman's contorted expression and stopped in his tracks. "Violet?" What were the odds she'd be here on his first assignment since moving to the area?

Next to none, but here she was. Directly in his path.

And in danger.

His Belgian Malinois growled.

"Wolf, hold." Maverick couldn't give the attack command until assessing the situation. He wouldn't make the mistake he'd made back at university. The mistake that had contributed to Violet's roommate's death. And right now, the same look of panic flashed in her eyes.

"Let. Her. Go." Maverick willed Constable Daley to reach them soon. Wolf had alerted to danger and zipped through the tree line. Maverick had followed. Sara was close behind.

He hoped.

"Not happening. Baylee has something I need." The man with the Santa hat sneered.

Baylee?

He had to save Violet. Maverick knew Wolf's abilities, but could Maverick get Violet to trust him after his brazen action to stop a shooter had failed miserably, and resulted in her roommate, Angie, getting shot? Something Maverick still wrestled with.

But he had to take the risk in order to save her. He caught Violet's gaze and gave her a slight signal of thrusting his elbow back. Would she understand his cue?

She blinked twice. He prayed that was her acknowledgment that she understood.

Movement behind them caught Santa Man's attention.

"Stand down," Sara yelled.

Violet elbowed the man and fell to her knees.

He staggered backward, giving Maverick the distraction he needed.

"Wolf, get 'em!" Maverick's command to his K-9 echoed throughout the area.

Wolf hurtled at lightning speed toward the masked man.

The suspect fired.

Wolf compensated his path to avoid the bullet, zigzagging.

Lord, don't let my dog get shot!

The K-9 leaped into the air and snatched the rifle in his mouth, knocking the suspect to the ground at the same time.

The man cursed and scrambled to his feet, then retreated into the forest, abandoning his weapon.

Sara reached the group. "Violet, are you okay?"

She nodded and pointed toward the trees. "Get him!"

The constable once again readied her Glock and bolted after the assailant.

Wolf trotted back to their side, the rifle still in his mouth. He dropped it beside Maverick.

"Good boy." Maverick brought out a reward from his bag and tossed it to the dog. Wolf snatched the treat, devouring it within seconds.

Maverick squatted beside Violet. "Did he hurt you?"

"No. What are you doing here?" Violet placed her gloved hands on the ground and pushed herself up. "Not that I'm ungrateful for you intervening, but I haven't seen you in years."

"I moved here two months ago to help start a new K-9 business at Hawkweed River Ranch." But that wasn't the entire reason. He pictured the five-year-old, red-haired girl living with him at the ranch. Riley. The daughter he'd been unaware of, whose trust he now struggled to earn. Becoming an instant father was not what he had planned. But that was a story for another time. Right now, he had a job to do.

Maverick tousled his dog's ears. "To answer your question, Violet, the mayor hired Wolf here to find remains in the park. I'm guessing you're the archeologist I'm to work with?"

"Yes." Her lips flattened for a split second before her expression changed. But not quick enough for him to miss the frustration on her face. She didn't like that he was here. Obviously, she still blamed him for Angie's death.

He swallowed back his regret. Not only would he prove Wolf's amazing abilities, but that Maverick had changed since university. He no longer made hasty decisions.

Angie's death had taught him that much.

"Violet, why did that man call you Baylee?"

"No idea, and he seemed to think I had something of his and

demanded it back." Violet eyed the dog and her eyes softened. "He's handsome. A Belgian Malinois, right?"

"I'm impressed. Some think Wolf's a German shepherd. They look similar."

"Love his name." Violet took a step forward, holding out her hand. "Hey, Wolf. Nice to meet you."

Sara returned and stowed her weapon. "Suspect is gone. Had an ATV waiting in a nearby clearing." She squatted in front of the rifle. "We'll get this dusted for prints, but I doubt we'll find any. He was wearing gloves." She gestured toward Wolf. "I'm impressed. How did you train him to find human remains and be a protector?"

"I used chemicals produced by corpses to train him on the scent of death, as well as other scents." Maverick bent and rubbed his K-9's back. "My brother and I also wanted to utilize Wolf's protection skills, similar to a police dog."

"So the best of both worlds." Sara adjusted her duty belt.

Violet shifted her stance. "Sara, you don't have a K-9 unit?"

"We do, but not an HRD dog. They're not in the budget, so that's why the mayor brought in Maverick and Wolf."

"How many remains has Wolf found?" Violet asked.

A question Maverick dreaded. "Many, mostly in training. This is his first official assignment here in Alberta. My brother, Austin, and I trained him back on the Murray K-9 Ranch."

Violet grimaced. "So, he technically hasn't found any remains. In the wild, so to speak."

"No, but he can, and will. If there are any here to find, of course."

A wind gust whisked through the trees, bringing with it a flurry of snowflakes. Maverick analyzed the weather conditions.

Darkened clouds had rolled in within the last hour. They had to act fast to get ahead of the storm approaching Asterbine National Park.

"Time to show you what Wolf can do." Maverick pointed to

the clouds. "Bad weather is moving in. Do you know where the remains could be?"

"Our intel said this location, but I used ground-penetrating radar around a wide perimeter. It didn't pick up a fourth skull or anything else." Violet dug out a map. "We need to expand our grid a bit more. Maybe to Hawkweed River." Violet folded her map and tucked it into her pack. "Time to work."

"Wolf, ready," Maverick commanded.

The dog hopped up onto all fours and barked.

"Wolf, seek."

The Malinois raised his snout in the air and circled, smelling each direction before hurtling off toward the tree line in an easterly direction.

"He's caught a scent. Let's follow." Maverick dashed after his K-9.

Fifteen minutes later, Maverick ducked under a cluster of trees and stepped into a rugged terrain close to cliffs.

Wolf barked and sat beside a rock formation, placing his paw on one end.

Maverick turned to Violet. "He's found something. That's his alert."

Violet approached the formation and peered over the cliff's edge. "Wow, that's a long way down. Stay back."

Sara's radio crackled.

"Daley, come in."

"That's my partner." She pressed the button. "Go ahead, Everett."

"Beware. Convict revealed someone is stalking archeologist Hoyt."

Violet pivoted, stumbling over a rock dangerously close to the edge.

Wolf barked and grabbed the bottom of her coat, tugging her backward.

Even before Maverick could act. "Whoa." He brought Violet into his arms. "You okay?"

"Wolf saved me from a possible tumble over the edge." She dropped beside the dog and hugged him. "Thank you."

Woof!

Violet stood and marched over to where Sara was standing. "What did this inmate say?"

The officer repeated her question over the radio.

"Said there's a bounty on the archeologist's head. Seems she's not who she says she is."

Violet's jaw dropped. "Sara, can I talk to him?"

The woman nodded and pressed the radio button, holding it up to Violet. "Nick, that's absurd. Where did he get that information?"

"That's all he knew." A hesitation filtered through the airwaves. "Daley, I just arrived at the dig site. Where are you exactly?"

Sara gave her partner the location where Wolf had alerted to remains.

"On my way."

"Copy that."

Violet picked up her device, passing it over the rock formation incrementally. Moments later, she scowled. "Gus isn't picking anything up."

Maverick raised his brow. "Gus?"

Violet lifted her tool. "Gus, the GPR."

He chuckled and knelt where Wolf had placed his paw, pushing on a large rock. "I trust my dog, not your device. No offense, but he can catch scents between rocks." He held out his hand. "Pass me your shovel."

She pursed her lips, but unclipped her folded shovel from her backpack before dropping beside him. "I'll dig. You and Sara clear the rocks."

"Where's Jill, Vi?" Sara asked.

"She had a family emergency but should be here soon." She lifted out a smaller rock and shoved it aside before digging.

Together, the group soon had a small opening cleared in the rock formation.

Violet dug carefully. Moments later, she stopped. "I grazed something. If it's what I think it is, we'll need to bring in our forensic anthropologist, Dr. Martin." Violet tossed the shovel aside and pulled out her brush, gingerly exposing what Wolf alerted to.

A skeleton.

"Well, I'll be." Violet glanced at Wolf. "Good boy."

Sara leaned closer. "But that's not a skull. Could this be the rest of the Hancocks' remains?"

"Possibly." Violet stood.

"I'll radio for Dr. Martin to come." Sara pressed her button and made the request with her dispatch.

"Thanks, Sara." Violet took out her camera. "I want to document—"

Wolf growled before barking, shifting his position. Something had caught the dog's attention.

Sara withdrew her weapon.

Maverick looked in the direction Wolf was facing.

A figure skulked in the forest as red flashed through the trees, followed by another.

Santa Man was back with reinforcements.

And they were perilously close to the cliff's edge.

With nowhere to run.

TWO

"Get behind the rocks!"

Violet's pulse zinged as she scampered to obey Sara's forceful command and ducked behind the skeletal grave they had unearthed.

Maverick followed and pointed to Violet. "Wolf, protect!"

The dog barked and positioned himself beside Violet in a tight formation, his gaze still directed toward the forest.

Violet peeked around the rocks. Two masked men wearing Santa hats emerged at the tree line. One lifted a bullhorn. "We only want the archeologist. Hand Baylee over, and we'll let you go."

A scream lodged in Violet's throat as her heart rate escalated, threatening to push her off the emotional roller coaster she rode.

Maverick wrapped a protective arm around her waist.

"Not happening. Stand down!" Sara squatted beside Maverick and Violet, weapon raised. "Everett, need backup," she whispered into her radio. "We're under attack. What's your ETA?"

"Almost there," the officer replied.

"You're outnumbered, Constable. Give her up." The other man with a Santa hat lifted his weapon. "Don't think that dog will save you this time. He makes one move and I shoot him."

Wolf growled.

Violet drew in a sharp breath. *Lord, protect us!*

"Daley, I've positioned myself behind the suspects." Nick's hushed voice came through Sara's radio. "I see a cave at your six. I'll distract the shooters and you get the others into the cave."

"Copy that."

"On three. One."

Violet noted the constable sneak to another tree.

Snowflakes intermingled with ice now hammered the region.

"Get ready to run, guys," Sara whispered.

"Two."

"We're waiting," Santa Man yelled. "You have five seconds to hand her over."

"Three. Now!" Constable Everett hurtled a stick toward the assailants. It thudded against a tree, the sound resonating.

The suspects pivoted.

"Run!" Sara's soft command spoke volumes.

Maverick took Violet's hand. "Let's go. Wolf, protect. Silent." He hauled her up and they crouch-ran toward the mountain.

Wolf barreled beside them, but remained quiet.

Gunfire erupted to their right, echoing throughout the mountainous area.

Violet grimaced at the sound, but refused to look back. She concentrated on getting to safety. She reached the opening, but slipped on the sleet-covered rocks.

Maverick caught her, preventing a fall, and nudged her inside the cave. "You okay?"

"Yes. Where's Sara? I thought she was behind us."

More shots answered Violet's question, followed by shouts.

"I'm guessing helping her partner fight off our attackers." Maverick turned on his flashlight, shining the beam around the cave. "Good, no bears are hibernating in here."

Pounding footfalls approached, elevating Violet's angst.

Maverick shoved her behind him. "Wolf, protect!"

The K-9 positioned himself at the entrance, growling.

"Just me, guys." Sara raised her hands. "Suspects escaped, and Everett is in pursuit."

"Wolf, out."

The dog retreated at Maverick's command.

Wolf's smarts impressed Violet. She wiped slush from her pants. "That was too close."

"Vi, do you have any idea who these people are? Why did they call you Baylee?" Sara holstered her weapon.

"No idea."

"Whoever they are, they sure are relentless." Maverick stroked Wolf's fur. "That's two attacks. What does the man think you have?"

She chewed on her lower lip. "Not sure. Sara, the man mentioned someone named Ragnovica earlier. Any idea who that is?"

Maverick's beam revealed the alarm on Sara's face. "Someone extremely dangerous. Why?"

"The man said I'm on that person's radar and shouldn't have removed the Hancock skulls." Violet hated that she'd been targeted for something she didn't do, but her find of the Hancock skulls had certainly put her in the spotlight after the *Asterbine Gazette* published a story on her and the archaeology dig. When they found the first skulls, the media had caught wind of the discovery and hounded Violet and her team relentlessly. "Have you heard of a Baylee Peck?" She took off her tuque and pried the elastic from her hair.

"No, but Asterbine Canyon isn't that big. I'm sure it wouldn't be difficult to locate her. If she lives in the area." Sara brought out a notebook and pen, scribbling on the page.

Constable Everett entered the cave, frowning. "Suspects escaped. They had ATVs waiting in a nearby clearing. You can come out now."

The group exited the cave.

"Good to see you again, Violet. Not under these conditions, of course." The constable stuck out his gloved hand toward Maverick. "I'm Constable Nick Everett, but call me Nick. You are?"

"K-9 handler Maverick Shaw. This is Wolf, my HRD dog."

"Good to meet you both."

"Maverick, I can't believe how high Wolf jumped earlier," Violet said.

"That was nothing. You should come to the ranch and I'll show you all his tricks."

The sleet stung Violet's face. "Nick, any word on when Dr. Martin will arrive? We need to get to work before the storm worsens."

"Last I heard, the anthropologist was en route with your colleague Jill." Nick motioned toward the half-exposed skeletal remains. "Could Amy Hancock's skull be hidden here?"

"Possibly. Not that I hope to find the eight-year-old's remains, but the mayor is pressuring my leader. Seems his daughter was best friends with Amy. Such a sad case." Violet turned to Maverick. "The Hancock family was brutally murdered, and we found three skulls last month. Amy is still unaccounted for."

Maverick's expression knotted. "That's horrible."

"Sure is, and with no further leads or evidence, we deemed it a cold case," Sara said. "I hated it came to that."

"Me, too. Amy's aunt has waited too long for both closure and justice." Violet kneeled in front of the crude burial site. "I need to clear the soil."

Maverick repositioned himself by Violet's side. "I can help you."

She didn't like the thought of asking for Maverick's assistance, but with the bad weather, she needed to work quickly. She didn't relish the idea of another attack in the secluded forest.

Violet had no choice but to accept his offer. Sure, she remembered how he'd reacted in the library years ago, but so far, she'd been impressed with this new, matured Maverick Shaw.

Not that she also hadn't made mistakes in the past.

Images of her mentor and fellow archeologist, Jesse Smith, watching her every move entered her mind. Even though it had been four years since their messy breakup, he still haunted her dreams. She'd fallen for Jesse fast and everything had been blissful until he ridiculed her in front of not only her colleagues but her friends. At first, she sloughed it off to her being sensitive, but when Sara mentioned it many times, Violet had to face the facts.

Not only had he made fun of her, but he continually grilled her about where she was, what she was doing and who she was with. A telltale sign of obsession, but she'd dismissed it, as she loved him deeply. However, Jesse Smith's fixation on Violet had escalated to stalking. He followed her around even after she'd broken up with him. She'd finally obtained a restraining order.

Even that hadn't deterred him.

She'd made the mistake of believing that Jesse loved her, and that had cost her dearly. Her hand flew to her stomach, where the evidence of his obsession remained carved on her abdomen.

A scar from Jesse's knife attack.

Her guilt over trusting him, even after all the warnings by family and friends, plagued her. Jesse had appeared so loving. She'd been duped.

Something she'd never let herself do again. Be fooled into falling in love.

Violet observed Maverick as he waited for her response. His long bang fell in front of his blue eyes. It had been years since they'd last seen each other, but his boy-next-door good looks had remained intact.

Not that she was looking.

"Fine. Thank you. I appreciate both of you helping." Violet addressed the constables. "Are we sure those men are gone? I need to concentrate and not be worrying about another attack."

"I saw them ride away," Nick said. "I've called in other constables to scour the area, though. Just to be sure."

"Thank you. That makes me feel better." Violet rechecked the sky. "Those dark clouds don't look good."

"Meteorologists are predicting five inches in the next few hours. At least there will be snow for Christmas." Maverick smiled his lopsided grin that had made the girls at university swoon. He had been the talk in the women's dorms.

Violet pushed away the memories of all her friends' crushes and concentrated on the task at hand. "Wouldn't be Christmas without snow. For me, anyway."

"Me, too. Tell me what you want me to do. Or is there another archeologist who can help?"

Jesse's handsome face flashed before her again. She stiffened her gloved fingers at her side. "No! We can do this." Violet hated the distress overtaking her normally cool and collected tone of voice.

Maverick's eyes widened. "Okay, then let's do this. Where do we start?"

Violet knew she'd probably have to explain her defensive answer, but right now she had a mission.

Find the rest of the remains and get out of the park.

Before the attackers returned.

Despite the chill moving into the mountain and wilderness area, Maverick wiped the sweat from his forehead. Working against the clock had not only made them rush, but added extra stress they didn't need. Thankfully, the suspects hadn't returned, and now Violet stood observing their find.

Three skeletal remains—minus their heads.

But no fourth skull.

Seemed the youngest Hancock child's disappearance remained a mystery. Questions plagued Maverick. Was little Amy Hancock really dead, or had someone abducted her? Or someone had hidden her from the criminal the masked man spoke about. Many possibilities.

Maverick stepped beside Violet. "Can you tell me more about this Ragnovica? I'm fairly new to the area and not up on all the news."

Nick's scowl shifted to his. "Not someone you want to mess with, that's for sure. Leader of a highly organized crime family."

"*Alleged* crime family," Sara added. "No one has obtained evidence to put them away, especially now that Don Hancock was murdered. He was about to testify against the Asterbine Shipping Company."

Maverick whistled. "Wow."

Sara's radio crackled and Dispatch asked her and Nick to report in. "Just a sec." She turned to them. "Gotta take this. We'll be at the edge of the tree line. Don't go anywhere. I'm trusting Wolf for your protection."

Wolf's ears flicked at the sound of his name, and he stood taller in protective mode.

"Good boy." Maverick tossed him another treat, showering his dog with a reward for a job well done. "What do you know about this shipping company, Violet?"

"Not much. Only rumors of them being a pipeline for illegal activity."

"What type of activity?"

"Drugs, money laundering, human trafficking... You name it, they've been accused of it." Violet squatted in front of the skeletons. "I wish we could find Amy Hancock."

"Does everyone feel she was killed, too?"

Violet's eyes clouded. "I'm afraid so. Police found multiple blood spatters in the Hancock home, but no bodies. Test results concluded the family's blood types were present. She's got to be here somewhere. I doubt they'd bury her far away. Makes no sense."

"Unless an animal got to her and dragged her somewhere else. Should we expand the grid?" Maverick petted his dog. "Get Wolf to keep searching?"

She stood. "I don't understand." She circled her index finger around the area. "This is where the inmate said the skull would be."

Sara returned. "Listen, Nick just left to escort Dr. Martin and Jill here, but we have to finish up soon."

"What's going on, Sara?" Violet asked.

"I hate to tell you this, but that inmate who helped us was just found stabbed to death."

Maverick didn't miss Violet's quick intake of breath. "Obviously, he paid the price for snitching."

"Yes, that's our guess, too, because there was a note sitting on his body."

Violet's jaw dropped. "What did it say?"

She clicked on her cell phone. "I'm quoting, 'This is what happens when you mess with Ragnovica. That archeologist is next.'"

"No!" Violet's knees buckled.

Maverick wrapped his arm around her waist, preventing a fall.

Wolf barked.

"Violet, you need to be in protective custody," Sara said.

Violet straightened and retreated from Maverick's hold. "I refuse to go into hiding. I have work to do. I must find Amy."

The wind strengthened, and the snowflakes intensified. It wouldn't be long before a heavy layer of snow blanketed the region. If that happened, Amy Hancock would be buried deeper. If she was even in Asterbine Park.

Riley entered Maverick's mind. Although he barely knew his daughter, her cuteness had quickly stolen his heart. If she was missing, he'd want them to do everything possible to find her. He agreed with Violet. They had to locate Amy.

It would give those who loved her closure.

"Time to send Wolf deeper into the forest. If Amy is here, he'll find her." Maverick focused on the constable. "Can you give us protection for the rest of the day?"

Sara pocketed her cell phone. "Violet, do you really think she's here?"

"Mayor Coble thinks so and is demanding closure for his daughter. She won't leave the house. He's concerned." Violet bit her lip. "If there's a chance Amy is in these woods, I have to take it."

Sara stuffed her hands into her pockets. "I admire your determination. Really, I do, but I'm concerned for your safety, my friend."

Clearly, the two women were close.

Violet placed her gloved hands on her hips. "I'm a Hoyt. Hoyts don't back down or leave a job unfinished."

Sara harrumphed. "Yes, I know. I've seen your stubborn streak and also met your sister Hazel a few summers ago in her park, remember? You both talk about your family, especially your father."

"He's tamed a lot since then. Please, Sara, let us do this. Christmas is almost here. I'd like to give the mayor's family and Amy's aunt the gift of closure. No matter what we find." She nodded toward Wolf. "Plus, we not only have you to protect us, but Wolf, too."

"Fine." Sara checked her watch. "It's now noon. I'll give you until four p.m. The weather is getting worse and we need to get off the mountain, especially because we'll lose daylight shortly after."

Violet scooped up her tools. "Thank you. Maverick, let's get Wolf searching."

"You got it." Maverick snapped his fingers. "Wolf, ready."

The dog stood at attention and barked.

Maverick pointed to the tree line. "Seek!"

The Malinois stormed toward the forest and leaped over a row of bushes, advancing into the woods.

"Come on." Maverick chased after his dog.

Violet and Sara followed as Sara shouted into her radio, giving her partner the direction of their pursuit.

Two hours later, after Dr. Colby Martin and Jill Mann had joined them, the group cleared the snow and dirt away from where Wolf had alerted. Nick had left to consult with the other constables scouring the park.

Working next to Violet brought back fond memories of their study sessions at the library. Only this time, Violet wasn't smiling but biting her lips at what she was about to unearth.

She finished clearing the soil and snow away, exposing the object of Wolf's alert.

A skull, with a few stringy long hairs still attached.

Violet inched closer and drew in a ragged, audible breath. "I doubt this is Amy. What do you think, Dr. Martin?"

"It's Colby, remember?" Dr. Martin examined the remains, taking his time before nodding. "Agreed. The skull is larger than a child's." He pointed toward the brow area. "The smaller forehead suggests female, though."

Violet sat back on her heels. "I wonder how long she's been buried."

Sara pointed to the skull. "The decapitation tells me it could be the same killer. The MO matches the Hancock family's murders."

Maverick tossed Wolf another reward. "Sara, do you have any reports of missing twentysomething females in the area?"

"None that I'm aware of."

Wolf growled seconds before movement behind them rustled the branches.

Violet jerked to her feet.

Maverick pushed her behind him. "Wolf, protect!"

The dog sprinted toward the noise.

Maverick held his breath, waiting for the possible masked man's return.

Two females appeared through the trees, raising their hands. "It's just us from the *Asterbine Gazette*," one of the women said. "Please have your dog stand down. We're only here for a story."

"Wolf, out!" Maverick commanded.

The dog retreated, moving beside Violet.

Sara rushed forward. "Remi, what are you doing here?"

"We heard you found more remains." She beckoned her cameraperson forward.

"How did you hear that?" Maverick asked.

"Police scanner. And you are?"

Sara positioned herself between Remi and Maverick. "None of your concern. You can't be here."

"This is a national park. I have every right." Remi turned to the cameraperson. "Debb, start rolling."

She focused the camera on Violet.

"Violet Hoyt, did you find the Hancock family?" Remi stuck the microphone in Violet's face.

Wolf growled.

Evidently, the Malinois didn't care for the reporter. *Good boy. Neither do I.*

"No comment," Violet said.

"Did you find Amy Hancock? The public wants to know."

"Again, no comment." Violet placed her gloved hand over the microphone. "Please, we have work to do." She returned to Dr. Martin's side.

"I also have it on good authority that you're not who you say you are."

Violet pivoted.

Once again, Wolf growled.

First, the masked man had called Violet by another name, and now this woman was questioning her identity.

The tortured expression on Violet's face told Maverick one thing.

She had no idea what the reporter was referring to.

THREE

Ice pellets mixed with the snow hammered the mountainous region, stinging Maverick's face. He scrutinized the black clouds rolling over the mountain peaks. Two inches had already fallen and more was coming. Time to get rid of this pesky reporter. He moved in front of Remi at the same time as Sara, creating a unified front. "Remi, is it? Please respect Ms. Hoyt and Constable Daley's wishes, and leave the area. The storm is getting worse, and we still have work to do." He flicked his hand at his K-9, giving him one of the silent commands he had taught him.

Intimidate.

Wolf growled and positioned himself directly in the reporter's path, baring his teeth.

"Whoa! Back down." Remi shuffled backward. "I'm only here for the truth. Please call that beast off."

Irritation steamed Maverick's face despite the cold temperature. The woman had hit a nerve. No one talked about his dog like that. "His name is Wolf, and if you're not careful, you may see exactly what he can do." His tone matched his dog's menacing stance.

Sara placed her hand on Maverick's arm. "Let's not be hasty." She spoke to the crew. "But he's right. You need to leave. If Ms. Hoyt wants to make a statement, she will contact you."

Remi's venomous expression shot toxic darts at Violet's back. "I want to know what she's hiding. I believe Asterbine Canyon would also be interested."

Violet whirled around. "I have no idea what you're talking

about. My name is Violet Erica Hoyt. What you see is what you get. Now, please, leave."

"I've heard Ragnovica has targeted you."

Wow. The woman was persistent. Maverick flicked his hand at Wolf again.

The dog growled his warning.

"Okay, that's enough." Sara clutched the reporter's arm and nudged her toward the clearing. "It really is time for you to leave or I'll charge you with trespassing." She shoved her. "Go! Both of you."

Remi raised her hands in surrender. "I'm going, but I will get the answers the public wants." Her eyes narrowed. "With or without your blessing." She stomped through the snow, the timid cameraperson following at her heels.

Sara huffed. "That was interesting. What in the world was she on about, Violet?"

Violet looked up from her position and shrugged. "First, that man called me Baylee, and now this."

"Maybe you have a twin—or a doppelgänger." Sara smirked.

"I highly doubt it." Violet stood. "Dr. Martin, we need to transport the head and other bones before the weather gets worse."

The man stood. "Agreed. Once I clean the bones at my lab, I'll give Dr. Welborn my findings. She'll then determine this female's identity and the cause of death. I can already tell you, though, as you suspected, this is not Amy Hancock."

Maverick studied the remains and grimaced as sadness swamped him. Who was this woman and did she have a family? He'd recently found his brother, Austin, after not knowing he had existed for most of his life. That had given him a renewed sense of how important family was. *Lord, why did you take this woman out of hers?* Maverick believed in God, but lately his faith had wavered. Sure, finding out about his brother had given him a refreshed purpose, but Maverick still had unresolved questions he found hard to compress: *Why doesn't God protect His flock? Why not answer prayers?*

"God answers, but we may not be listening, or we just don't like His response," Austin had told him once.

"I realize your team deemed this entire area an archeological site, but I'm calling it a crime scene. I'm contacting some constables to come and guard it until the remains can be extracted." Sara lifted her radio. "We can't have thieves or animals disturbing evidence. Plus, I'm getting Violet an escort."

"I don't require protection, Sara." Violet's neck veins visibly pulsated before she averted her gaze and stuffed her tools into her backpack. "I'm fine."

Her expression and tense tone of voice told Maverick one thing. She was anything but fine.

He recognized that look from their university days. Violet Hoyt was terrified.

An idea formed, but it would take some convincing on his behalf. He realized he was treading on thin ice with Violet. She still didn't trust him. "Violet, please hear me out."

She tilted her head and placed her hands on her hips. "What?"

"You need protection, as Sara is suggesting, so how about you come and stay at Hawkweed River Ranch? It's not that far from this park and there's lots of room."

"No. My condo has a great security system."

Sara's lips twisted into a scowl. "If you won't let us guard you, please go to the ranch. I know the owner and they have ex-military working there as ranch hands. They know how to keep someone safe. Besides, I'm familiar with your father's protective nature. I don't need the wrath of Frank Hoyt coming down on me."

Maverick silently thanked the constable for agreeing with his suggestion. "Please come. The ranch is all decked out for Christmas and I remember how much you love this time of year."

Violet's eyes brightened.

Gotcha. Maverick figured that would pique her interest.

"Fine. You know me too well. I want to go to my condo first and pack a few clothes. And call my mom."

"Good. I'm gonna get those constables here." Sara spoke into her radio, wandering a few feet away.

After two constables secured the site and Dr. Martin made arrangements for the transport of the victim's head and the other bones, the team began their trek back down the mountain through the slick conditions. They returned to their earlier meeting location and found their ATVs covered in snow and ice. The storm had blanketed the region with five inches of snow.

"Oh, dear. The drive back on our ATVs should be interesting." Violet obviously had the same thought as he did.

The hazardous trails they had traveled on earlier would be even more dicey.

"We'll be fine," Sara said. "The tires are thick. Time to get going. Dusk will soon change to complete darkness."

The team advanced to their vehicle and simultaneously halted in their tracks.

Someone had slashed all their tires.

Getting to the park station before dark would now be impossible. The bigger question forming in Maverick's mind sent his heart hammering.

Was the tire slasher hovering nearby, watching their every move?

Violet's pulse throbbed as she noted Sara's wrenched expression and the constable casually placed her hand on her weapon. "Sara, do you think whoever did this is still in the area?"

"Possibly, and I'm not taking any risks." Sara removed her Maglite and shone it around the region. When nothing materialized, she pressed her radio button. "Everett, come in."

Seconds later, Nick responded. "Report. You off the mountain?"

"Yes, but someone slashed all our ATV tires. How far out are you?"

"Under a click. Any sign of the suspect?"

Sara kicked at her ATV's tire. "None. We need transport."

Wolf growled.

An engine's roar sounded in the distance.

Someone was coming.

The Malinois barked.

"Everyone, get behind me." Sara unholstered her weapon. "Everett, is that you approaching us?"

"No. Take cover! ETA is two minutes."

"Copy." Sara pointed to the trees. "Get over there. Now!"

The team scrambled to the Balsam firs to get out of the approaching suspect's path.

Not again! Violet's heartbeat threatened to explode out of her chest. How many times would they be attacked in one day? *Deep breaths, Vi.* She inhaled, then exhaled slowly to regulate her breathing. She repeated the process. *God, I don't need any more excitement today. My heart can't take it.*

She'd recently been diagnosed with an irregular heart rhythm. Stress and too much caffeine not only increased her heart rate but elevated her blood pressure. She'd switched to decaf when she received the news of her heart, but right now, with the day's events, her stress was high enough to jeopardize her health.

Lights flashed through the trees as a snowmobile roared into the area and stopped at the tree line. Santa Man raised an enormous weapon and, seconds later, a streak of light illuminated the sky.

"RPG! Get down," Sara yelled, firing her Glock.

The rocket-propelled grenade careened toward them.

Maverick hauled Violet to the ground. "Wolf, protect!"

The dog positioned himself in front of Maverick and Violet, acting as their sentinel.

Lord, protect us!

An explosion blasted next to Dr. Martin, launching him into the air. He thudded against a tree and landed a few feet from Violet.

"Colby!" She crouch-walked to his position.

His eyelids fluttered open.

Moments later, another engine roared, and a second snowmobile appeared around the corner. Constable Everett.

The gunman sped away.

Violet examined Dr. Martin's injuries, her heart now in full panic mode. "Stay with me. Sara, we need EMS. Now!"

The constable yelled into her radio, requesting assistance, and stated their location.

"Daley, a park warden is on the way with help to get you all back to their station." Nick's voice came through Sara's radio. "Can you transport the doctor there? It would make it easier for EMS to reach him."

"Violet, how is he?" Sara asked.

Violet checked his vitals. "Weakening. We're running out of time."

"I'm going after this suspect," Nick yelled. "We're gonna lose him if I don't."

Sara pressed her button. "Copy."

Nick pursued the assailant, and he disappeared around the corner.

"Violet, I'm not…" Dr. Martin's voice trailed off.

"Colby, don't talk." Violet pressed harder.

He lifted his limp hand. "Not—going—to—make it. Watch—your—back with Dr. Patch."

His fellow forensic anthropologist.

She tensed. Why would he give that warning? She patted his arm. "You're going to be okay."

"No, I—give you—permission to proceed. Find—Amy. She—" His hand plopped down, and he stilled.

"No! Sara, where is the park warden?"

The constable took off her glove and felt for a pulse. "I'm sorry, Vi. He's gone." She stood from her position. "Do you see why you need protection?"

Tears formed at the loss of her colleague. Violet acknowledged that fact and nodded.

Someone had definitely targeted her, and now Dr. Martin was dead. She'd put them all at risk.

Fifteen minutes later, multiple vehicles approached. The park warden and his crew had arrived to take them back. Maverick helped the warden place Dr. Martin in the back of one of their sleds. Deep regret over the anthropologist's death sat on Violet's chest. *Lord, be with his family.* It was difficult to lose someone, but even harder during the Christmas season.

Nick had reported that unfortunately Santa Man had cut him off, causing Nick's snowmobile to capsize before the suspect sped away.

After being transported to her SUV, Violet drove home, with Maverick and Wolf close behind. Sara also followed, giving them added protection. She was a friend and wouldn't let Violet take this trip alone.

When Violet pulled into her driveway, Sara tapped on her car window and waited for Violet to open it. "Give me your keys. I want to clear your condo first."

"Is that really necessary? I have Wolf to protect me. You've had a long day. Go home, Sara." Violet hated being a nuisance.

Her friend wiggled her gloved fingers. "After what happened to Dr. Martin? Nope. Come on. Pass them to me."

Violet relented and dropped her keys into Sara's hand.

Seven minutes later, Sara waved them in.

Violet waited for Maverick to exit his vehicle. He released Wolf from his cage and the duo approached.

"I'm so sorry for your loss," Maverick said. "Did you know Dr. Martin well?"

"A little. He was always so kind."

"What did he mean about this Dr. Patch?"

Watch your back.

Dr. Martin's words about his colleague baffled Violet. "Not sure."

"Let's get you inside." Maverick nudged her forward.

Violet's shoulders slumped. She could hardly believe she'd

consented to this absurd idea of staying with him at the ranch. But at least there, she could roam around. Surely no one would attack with all their employees hovering about. Right?

Violet silenced her questions and hurried toward her front door. Time to get this done. She squared her posture, determination setting in, and entered her home with her entourage.

Her orange tabby meowed and wrapped herself around Violet's ankles. She squatted. "Marmalade, you love me, don't you?"

She meowed.

The cat's affection was the medicine Violet required right now. She picked her up and brought the lovable tabby to her face, kissing her. "You knew I needed that, didn't you?"

"Who do we have here?" Maverick kneeled beside Violet and took off his gloves, holding out his fingers.

Wolf barked.

Marmalade hissed and scattered from Violet's hold, running under the nearby couch.

"Clearly, Marmy doesn't like Wolf." Violet pushed herself to her feet. "Who's going to take care of her?"

"Bring her. Riley loves cats."

Riley? Was that his wife? Violet eyed his left ring finger. Empty. Why did she even care? The secret crush she'd had on him at university reemerged. "Riley?"

"My daughter."

Her mouth dropped. "Wait, you have a daughter?"

"Yes, she's five. I'll tell you more later." He pushed himself up. "Time for you to call your mom and pack."

Violet ignored the silent questions tumbling through her mind and turned to Sara. "You can go now. I'm pretty sure whoever attacked us doesn't know where I live and you made sure no one followed us."

The constable pointed. "You do as the man said and pack."

"Yes, ma'am." Violet saluted her friend, wiggled out of her coat and tossed it onto a nearby chair. "I won't be long. Sara, can you grab Marmy's food? You know where it is."

She nodded. "I'll get the cage, too."

"I'll try to coax your cat out from under the couch." Maverick took off his hiking boots and entered the living room.

Violet dug her phone from her bag and selected her mother's number as she entered her bedroom.

Erica Hoyt answered on the second ring. "Hey, little lady. How are you?"

Violet put her mom on speaker and tossed her cell phone onto the bed. "I've been better, Mom." She kneeled in front of her bed and dug out her suitcase.

"What's wrong?" Concern laced her mom's voice.

"Let's just say it's been an interesting day." As she stuffed clothes into her suitcase, Violet shared some of the events with her mother and informed her that she was heading to Maverick's ranch.

"Are you okay? I'm so sorry about your friend's death. I can leave right now."

No, she wouldn't put her mother at risk. Besides, their relationship had been testy lately, and Violet couldn't deal with her sometimes smothering Mama Bear personality. "Mom, I'll be fine. Listen, do you know a Baylee Peck?"

"No, why?"

"Because that's what the assailant called me." She chuckled. "Sara thinks I must have a twin or something."

Silence.

Violet stopped packing. "Mom, you there?"

Nothing.

Violet checked her phone. Still connected. What was going on? "Mom, why aren't you answering?"

"You better sit down for this." Her mother's whispered words elevated Violet's stress.

She plunked onto her bed. "What is it?"

"I never told you or the others this, but you weren't our firstborn daughter."

Violet froze. "What are you talking about, Mom?"

An elongated exhale filtered through the phone. "I was pregnant with twins. Your sister came out first, but the doctor whisked her away, stating her heart wasn't beating. Then you came out next."

What? Violet clamped her eyes shut at her mother's news. "What happened to my sister?"

"She died, Vi. The doctor failed to revive her."

Anger flushed Violet's cheeks. "And you kept this from me all these years? Why?" She dug her nails into her palms to curb her irritation at her mother.

"Because I didn't believe it was necessary to put you through the pain of knowing your twin had passed."

The empty feeling Violet had as a child resurfaced. Could she have somehow sensed the twin sharing their mother's womb had died? Wait—

Violet snagged her phone and bolted to her feet. "Mom, are you sure she died?"

"Yes. I have the death certificate."

The assailant's words from earlier today resurfaced, cementing Violet in place.

You can't fool me, Violet Hoyt. I know who you really are, Baylee Peck.

Was her sister alive?

"Vi, why would you ask that?"

"Because I don't think she died, Mom." She told her what the man had said at the dig site.

A loud intake of breath blasted through the phone. "Impossible."

Was it? The man thought Violet was Baylee. In fact, he seemed sure of it. Realization dawned on Violet.

Her sister was alive.

Wolf barked.

A crash sounded seconds later, followed by a gunshot.

Violet dropped her phone.

Someone had breached her home.

FOUR

Maverick shuddered as a vise clamped his heart, stealing his mobility. Wolf barked and growled seconds before Santa Man crashed through the condo's front door, firing a shot into the foyer. Thankfully, it missed any mark. Multiple pounding footfalls told Maverick both females were approaching. "Vi, stay away!"

Wolf continued to bark ferociously. The man halted inside the hallway.

Sara appeared around the corner, gun raised. "Police, stand down!"

Santa Man fired another shot. The bullet lodged into the wall, narrowly missing Sara's head. She fired back.

The distraction gave Maverick the opportunity to unleash his own weapon. "Wolf, get 'em!"

Wolf leaped into the air and crashed into the assailant, knocking him down. His gun clattered onto the floor in the foyer.

Violet edged around the corner.

"Vi, stay back." Sara kicked the gun out of Santa Man's reach. She aimed her Glock at him. "Stay down if you know what's good for you." Her raised voice spoke volumes.

Wolf kept his front paws on top of the suspect, growling and baring his teeth.

The man grunted. "Get that dog away from me."

"I've got this, Maverick," Sara said.

"Wolf, out," he commanded. "Stay." Maverick would not risk him getting away again. Violet's and Sara's lives were still in danger.

And Maverick refused to let history repeat itself, especially after what had happened to Angie. Images of the gunman flashed, and Maverick couldn't block the scene from his mind.

Maverick, Violet and Angie had been studying together in the university library when the student barged into the room waving his rifle. The three of them had sprung to their feet simultaneously as the man aimed his weapon at Violet.

Maverick had panicked and plowed into him to save the girls, but the rifle had discharged and the stray bullet hit Angie directly in the chest. She died five minutes later in Violet's arms.

Maverick's foolish, brazen action had killed Violet's best friend.

And Violet's expression had told him everything. She blamed Maverick for taking matters into his own hands.

Some hero he turned out to be. That one attempted act of heroism had cost him everything. Violet's friendship and any relationship he had secretly longed for. Even though Maverick had dated other women, he had a crush on Violet Hoyt.

"Maverick, did you hear me?" Violet's raised question brought him back into the present.

"Sorry, what did you say?"

"Sara asked you to watch for the constables that are en route." She grabbed his arm. "Where did you just go? You okay?"

"Fine. Just memories."

Her eyes clouded, and she released his arm. "Let's not go there. Not here. Not now."

The tone in her voice told him she knew exactly what memory he referred to, and she still blamed him for Angie's death.

He agreed. The guilt over that day still haunted him. Even after the police had apprehended and charged the shooter with Angie's murder.

It was almost as if Maverick had pulled the trigger in that library. He slouched and walked to the broken door, peering out into the darkness. Snow continued to fall, adding to the trepidation already flowing through his body. The weather conditions weren't helping their situation.

Sara handcuffed Santa Man and hauled him to his feet, then shoved him into a nearby chair.

He grunted. "Take it easy."

Violet marched over to the man. "Take it easy? You just tried to kill us. Again. That's four times today." She yanked off his Santa hat and dragged his mask down. She staggered backward.

Tattoos splattered over the man's face, but Maverick guessed that wasn't what had caught Violet off guard. It was the deep scars trailing overtop of his right eye down to his chin.

"Who—who—are—you?" Violet's broken question revealed her surprise and panic.

Santa Man spat. "You can't fool me, Baylee. You told me you loved me, scars and all."

"I. Don't. Know. You."

Wolf growled at Violet's raised tone, moving closer to her side.

Maverick had trained his dog well. The Malinois not only could find remains but was well-versed in protective detail and sensed her fear.

"How can you say that, Baylee?" Santa Man shifted in the chair.

Violet threw her hands in the air. "How many times do I need to tell you? I'm not Baylee. I'm Violet Hoyt."

His expression contorted seconds before his eyes darkened. "You betrayed me and, for that, you'll pay. Ragnovica knows you stole from me. You're on their radar now, too. Trust me, you can't escape. Their clutches run deep."

Sara gently nudged Violet away and addressed the man. "Tell me your name."

"I ain't tellin' you squat."

Wolf growled.

"Who is Ragnovica?" Sara continued to drill the man.

"Someone you don't want to mess with." He shifted his attention to Violet. "And you better watch your back, missy. You have something they want."

Maverick didn't miss the flash of terror on Violet's face. "What is it she supposedly has?"

"Who are you? I assume you own this beast?" He motioned toward Wolf.

"I do, and *you* better watch *your* back. Wolf is a fierce protector."

The Malinois bared his teeth at Maverick's heightened octave. *Good boy.*

Sirens blared nearby, announcing their backup.

Sara raised her hand in a stop position directed at Maverick. "I can handle this. You let the constables in."

Santa Man sneered. "Copper, you ain't getting anything from me. I want a lawyer." He clamped his lips shut.

Maverick suppressed the grunt of frustration he wanted to expel. "Vi, finish packing. Time to leave." He prodded over to the door and shoved the broken wood away, beckoning the constables inside.

Evidently, this man wasn't going to give them any information that would help stop Ragnovica. Two questions remained in Maverick's mind.

Who was Ragnovica, and what object did they think Violet had?

One thing he knew for sure… Maverick had to get her to the ranch quickly to hide her.

And keep her alive.

Violet rested her head against the passenger seat of Maverick's SUV. Constables had taken Santa Man away an hour ago. Violet inhaled slowly and exhaled, counting to five. Her heart rate had been on a turbulent ride since she found out Baylee was her twin, and the episode with the intruder hadn't helped. Violet willed her heart's rhythm to slow down.

She turned to glance at Marmalade, who was riding with

them in her carry-on cage. Just before they left Violet's condo, they'd found the cat hiding behind the couch. Marmy was the only normal thing in her life at the moment. And right now she needed normal, after the way her world had turned topsy-turvy.

"You okay?" Maverick made a right onto the highway that would take them to Hawkweed River Ranch.

She puffed out a breath. "I will be when this is all over."

"What did you find out from your mom?"

Violet gritted her teeth as she thought back to her conversation with Erica Hoyt. "It seems my mother has been keeping secrets from all of us children." She hesitated, letting what she was about to say sink in. "I have a twin sister."

His gaze snapped to hers. "What? She never told you that?"

"Nope. In her defense, the doctor said her first daughter died with heart complications." Interesting. Could Baylee really have heart issues like Violet?

"Why wouldn't she tell you, though?"

"She claims she didn't want to make us sad."

"I guess that kind of makes sense, but still hard for you to find out now. This way."

"Yup. The Hoyts have been through so much. My brother Kyle committed suicide at age twelve. Dad has been kidnapped twice. Recently, my brother Dekker was targeted by a serial killer."

"What? I remember you telling me about Kyle, but no family should have to go through all that."

"That's not the half of it, but Mom still should have told me." Violet had always been close to her mother. Until recently. They had been at odds over some of Violet's life choices. Mainly, her wavering faith in God. And now this news had muddied their relationship even more.

"I'm sure she only wanted to protect you."

"You mean smother me." Recently, Erica Hoyt had shown a tendency to do that, and Violet was tired of it. She hissed out a breath. "Sorry, I need sleep and don't mean to sound horrible.

Don't get me wrong. I love my mother to the moon and back, but she's been inserting her opinions about everything I do lately."

Maverick averted his eyes, but not before she caught tears glistening.

"I'm sorry. I didn't mean to sound harsh."

"No, it's not that. My mom passed a couple years ago and right now, I'd give anything to hear her voice."

Violet bit the inside of her mouth. *Way to go, Vi.* She immediately regretted her two-year-old tantrum. *Get a grip.* "I'm so sorry about your mom."

"Thank you. It was after her death that I found out about my brother, Austin. Long story, but my parents had kept the fact that I had a brother a secret from me, too, so I can relate to your frustration. As they say, been there, done that."

Violet reached over and grazed his hand on the steering wheel. "That's tough. How's your relationship with your brother?"

"Rocky at first, but solid now. I admire him. He's why I'm going into the K-9 training business. I've always loved dogs, but watching him train his has instilled the desire to do more with my life. Plus, he said training dogs came naturally to me." Maverick turned down a countryside road. "That's what brought me to Hawkweed River Ranch. The owner reached out to Austin to find out how to start a K-9 training facility. Through our discussions, I found out that he was also looking to sell. Mom had left me and Austin a sizable insurance policy, so we're buying the ranch."

"That's amazing." She studied his profile. His wavy blond hair had always been her kryptonite when it came to Maverick Shaw. She had resisted the urge to run her fingers through it many times, especially when his long bang fell over his eyes while studying at the library. She'd seen the way other girls drooled over the handsome student. His cute charm had captured the attention of all her friends.

Including herself, but she had tucked her crush away as he

dated others. He obviously hadn't thought of her as anything but a friend.

And after Angie's death, he distanced himself, and their friendship had ended. Sure, she had initially blamed him for her friend's death. His rush to act had been reckless, but would the gunman have killed anyway?

Police had informed them later that the student confessed to hating certain members of their class and vowed revenge. He had entered the library with the intent of making some of them pay for betraying him.

Violet flinched at the secret she still held from that night. A secret she'd regretted and been foolish to keep, but now it was too late.

Maverick's SUV swerved on a patch of black ice, thrusting her thoughts back to the present.

Wolf barked.

Violet's pulse increased, and she clung to the armrest.

Maverick compensated, and the vehicle righted itself. "Sorry, didn't see that ice patch."

"That was close." Violet looked out the windshield. The snow had intensified over the past few hours, dumping another five inches throughout the area. "The joys of winter in Alberta. We've been fortunate so far, though. This is our first major snowstorm. The roads are getting worse. Looks like tomorrow may be a work-from-home day. I just hope Dr. Patch and the forensic team extracted the remains off the mountain."

"She hasn't let you know?"

Violet fished out her cell phone. "No, and it's now ten o'clock. I'm going to text her." She tapped on her phone and sent the message.

A reply came within a minute.

On my way to the lab now. Call me. I don't do texts.

Dr. Martin's last words replayed in her mind. "No wonder Colby warned me to watch my back with her. Something tells me she doesn't like me." She read the text out loud. "Guess I've been told, huh?"

Maverick whistled. "Yup." He hit his signal light. "We're here." He stopped in front of a gate and tapped on his phone sitting in its dash holder. The gate doors rolled open.

He drove down a long driveway connecting the road to the Hawkweed River Ranch.

Moments later, he parked in front of a large, log-style ranch decorated for Christmas. Multicolored lights adorned the eaves troughs and veranda railings as well as the red barn to the right. The tall Balsam fir decked out with similar lights and oversized Christmas balls also added to the festive appearance.

"Wow. This is beautiful. You own all this?"

"Not yet. Austin and I will co-own it when the deal goes through." He cut the engine. "He's coming for a visit. We'll sign the final paperwork then."

"That's amazing."

"Shall we head inside? I'll show you to your room so you can make that phone call in private." He opened his door and went to the rear to release Wolf from his cage.

Violet climbed out and lifted Marmalade from the back seat. She meowed. "You're okay, Marmy. Welcome to your new temporary home."

She meowed a second time.

Violet chuckled before following Maverick and Wolf up the veranda steps, avoiding patches of snow. They entered the ranch, and Violet stomped the snow from her boots.

A redheaded girl dressed in Christmas pajamas skipped into the hallway, carrying a stuffed bunny. She skidded to a stop when she saw Violet.

Her jaw dropped. "Mama?"

What in the world? Why did this little girl think Violet was her mother?

FIVE

Maverick didn't miss the alarm on Violet's face. She resembled Piper, Riley's mother, except Piper's hair had a reddish tone to it and Violet was much prettier. Not that he was looking for any relationship—other than one with his newfound daughter. And right now, that relationship was shaky. The little girl didn't trust him. Not that Maverick blamed her. The car crash had taken her mother instantly, leaving her with a man she didn't know. He had to earn her trust.

Maverick squatted in front of Riley. "Pumpkin, this is my friend Violet Hoyt. Remember, Mommy isn't here anymore but is watching over you. She's in here." Maverick placed his hand over Riley's heart.

"No!" Riley sulked.

"I'm sorry. Daddy loves you."

She scowled and threw the bunny on the floor. "You're not my daddy." She marched over to Violet and hugged her leg.

"Oomph." Violet let out a soft gulp.

Maverick pushed himself up, silencing the sigh sitting on the tip of his tongue. He mouthed, "Sorry," to Violet.

"Riley, where did you go?" The ranch owner's cook scurried into the foyer, panting for breaths. "There you are. Sorry, Maverick, she got away from me."

"No problem. I'm back now, so you can leave. I appreciate you looking after her."

The woman nodded and retreated to the kitchen.

Wolf bounded around the group and barreled after her. He

wanted to be fed, but right now, Maverick had to tend to his daughter.

"Riley, say hi to Violet and then it's time for bed."

She stomped her foot. "No!"

Violet set Marmalade down. "Would you like to meet my cat, Riley?"

Riley's eyes brightened. "Yes."

Violet opened the door and gathered her cat in her arms. "Riley, this is Marmalade."

Riley rubbed the feline's fur. "She's so soft." She turned up her nose. "But marm-u-lade is for toast."

Violet laughed. "I named her that because she's orange like marmalade. I call her Marmy."

The cat's ears twitched as if she realized they were talking about her. She nestled into Riley's touch.

"She likes you, Pumpkin."

"I don't want to go to bed. Can I play with her?" Her wide blue eyes pleaded with Maverick.

"It's late and you need sleep. Remember, Santa comes soon."

Her bottom lip protruded, and she crossed her arms.

Violet leaned closer. "How about I let Marmy sleep with you? That okay, Maverick?"

The child's pupils grew the size of saucers, and she tugged on Maverick's arm. "Can I, mister?"

Mister?

"Sure." Anything to please his daughter and get her one step closer to trusting him.

Riley bounced up and down. "Goody!" She scooped her bunny from the floor. "Come on, Marmy. Let's go to bed." She skittered toward the spiral log steps but turned, raising the stuffed animal. "Oh, Marmy, this is Hoppy."

Violet picked up her cat. "Marmy says hi to Hoppy." She leaned closer to Maverick. "You okay if I tuck her in?"

"Of course. I think you've already won her friendship. Wish I could say the same."

Violet's expression softened. "How about you put on the kettle and we can chat? I want to find out more about Riley. After I make a quick call to Dr. Patch."

"Sounds good. The guest bedroom is beside Riley's. The one decked out in buffalo plaid." He snickered. "You can't miss it."

"Be back soon."

"I'll see you in the kitchen. It's that way." He pointed to the right. "I need to feed Wolf and reconnect with Austin."

She nodded before bounding up the stairs after Riley.

God, if You're listening, please help my daughter learn to love me.

Maverick meandered into the kitchen as thoughts tumbled through his mind. He had given his life over to God by watching his brother's faith play out. Their mother had taught Maverick about God, but he'd been stubborn in surrendering. Even after what Austin went through while protecting his wife, Izzy, Austin's faith was steadfast, and that had impressed Maverick. The man lived out what he believed, and Maverick had wanted that.

However, his own faith in God had been tested when he received a phone call from the police requesting he pick up his daughter at the police station. A daughter his ex-girlfriend had failed to mention.

Why would God withhold the joy of his child for five whole years? Maverick was smitten the first time he laid eyes on the cutest redhead he'd ever seen. Freckles and all.

Now, if only Riley would settle in her new life on Hawkweed River Ranch.

Woof!

Maverick's bark reminded him of why he came into the kitchen. "I'm coming, boy." He withdrew the dog's food from the cupboard and filled Wolf's dish before pouring water in the other one. "There you go. You deserve a good meal." He rubbed his dog's back and kissed him on the head. "You're amazing."

His K-9 woofed again before devouring his food.

Maverick unclipped his cell phone and chose Austin's number from his contact list, placing the call on speaker. He set his phone on the kitchen island.

Austin answered on the second ring. "Hey, Mav. How did it go with the archeologist? Wolf alert to anything?"

"Just got back to the ranch, and yes, he sure did. Let's just say it's been an interesting day."

"What happened?"

Maverick lifted the teakettle off the stove and filled it with water as he relayed the day's events.

Austin whistled. "Oh, my. Are you okay?"

"Fine. Wolf sure made me proud."

"Well, we trained him hard, and it's paid off, so—" A dog's bark interrupted his sentence. "Névé says hi."

"I miss her. You and Izzy, too, of course." Maverick chuckled and pulled two mugs out of the cupboard. "You still coming for a visit?"

"You betcha. I want to meet my new niece. Tell me about Violet, and are you sure you're well protected there? I'm concerned that you're also now on this Ragnovica's radar. Good thing Izzy is coming, too."

"Some of the ranch hands are ex-military and very capable. I called Buck before we came, to ensure that it was okay to bring Violet. I haven't seen him yet, but he's probably over at the ranch cabins updating the others."

"Good. That makes me feel better. Not that you don't know how to use a rifle or anything."

Maverick observed his dog. "That and a powerful Malinois."

"True. So, have you met this Violet before?"

Right, Maverick had never told his brother about her. "Long story." He quickly gave him the details of how they'd met and what happened back in his university days. "Riley seems to have warmed up to her already. Just wish my daughter would open up to me, too."

"Mav, it's only been a couple of months. Five years without a dad is long for a child. You need to give her time. Let her see the man Izzy and I love. The man who cares deeply for those around him. God will show you."

The kettle whistled as Violet appeared in the doorway.

"I gotta run. Can't wait to see you. Bring Névé with you." He poured the hot water into two mugs.

"Will do. See you soon." Austin ended the call.

Maverick unwrapped two tea bags as Violet entered. He held one up. "Chamomile okay?"

"Sounds wonderful. Riley is already asleep, and Marmy is curled up on the pillow beside her. Her favorite spot to snuggle."

He handed her a mug. "Let's sit at the table."

She complied. "You get in touch with your brother?"

"Sure did. Hey, Wolf, Névé is coming for a visit."

The dog barked.

"Névé?" Violet dunked the bag.

"Austin's malamute and Wolf's friend." He sat across from Violet. "Thank you for helping with Riley."

"My pleasure. She's adorable, but why would she think I was her mother?"

"You resemble Piper a bit, but your hair is darker."

She raised a brow. "Interesting. Tell me about her and Riley."

Maverick lifted out the tea bag and set it on a plate beside him as he gathered his thoughts. How much of that period of his life should he divulge? It was after university and he still hadn't dealt with the guilt of what happened to Angie. He wasn't proud of himself. Of the way he acted around people. His cocky attitude had often got him into trouble.

He sipped his tea and wrapped his hands around the mug, the warmth spreading into his chilled bones. "It's late, so I'll make a long story short. First, did you call Dr. Patch?"

"She didn't pick up. Probably either really busy or ignoring me. I left a message." She took a drink. "So good. Wait, do you have any cookies? I haven't eaten since breakfast and I'm starved."

Maverick hopped to his feet. "Ah, your sugar fetish. I should have remembered. Just a sec." He brought out a snowman jar from the pantry. "Buck's cook always leaves cookies, and she made gingerbread ones with Riley yesterday." He placed it on the table and opened the lid. "Help yourself."

She nabbed one and stuffed it into her mouth, mumbling, "Thank you." She swallowed. "Okay, ready now. Go ahead."

"Shortly after we graduated from university, I kind of went on a bingeing spree I'm not proud of."

"What do you mean?"

"Socializing and out all the time, neglecting family and my responsibilities. Dating."

"You were young. No one can blame you for that." Violet sipped her tea.

If she heard the entire story, she may not dismiss his actions so easily. "Six and a half years ago, I met Piper. Riley's mom. I was at a point in my life when I really didn't know what I wanted to do…and I was still struggling over Angie's death."

He noted her twisted lips and narrowed eyes.

A subject she obviously didn't want to talk about.

"Anyway, her take-charge attitude lured me in and I fell hard for her. Her friends became my friends. I ignored mine, much to my mother's dismay. You can guess where that led."

He snatched a cookie to give himself a break from the bad memories, taking his time chewing before he washed it down with tea.

"Mav, we've all done things in our lives we're not proud of. I'm not here to judge."

"That means a lot. I've grown up since that time in my life." He took another sip. "Six months into our relationship, I got fired. My boss claimed I'd changed and not for the good. My mother and father tried to convince me to break up with Piper. They saw she was toxic, but I couldn't see it. I was that far gone. It took getting fired to make me finally see that I had let Piper rule every aspect of my life. I knew it was time to stand up to her."

"What happened?"

"I confronted her and said that we had to make changes.

She seemed to agree, but after I returned the next day from job searching, she was gone. No note. No phone call. Nothing. She'd cleaned out her closet." Not the entire story, but enough for now.

Violet's jaw dropped. "You never heard from her again?"

"Nope. I didn't even know she was pregnant. Just over two months ago, the police called Austin's ranch looking for me. They said I had a child and to come claim her at their police station."

"What? That's horrible." She reached across the table and placed her hand on his. "I'm so sorry."

"Thank you. I became an instant dad. Apparently, Piper's parents had passed away, and she had no other family. Police found out about me from Riley's birth certificate." He huffed. "At least Piper had the decency to name me as the father."

"Wow. I feel so bad for you and Riley. Becoming an instant family is tough on both."

He finished his tea and took his mug to the sink. "It is, and Riley has had a hard time adjusting. I'm really hoping Christmas will bring her around and make her happy."

"Mav, you don't need Christmas. You only need to show her you love her and care for her."

"True, but a few presents may help." He chuckled. "I know... I can't buy her love. I just—"

The alarm system announced the front door had opened at the same time as Violet's cell phone buzzed.

"That must be the ranch owner, Buck, returning."

Violet stood and checked her phone. "And this is Dr. Patch. Is there somewhere I can take this in private?"

He pointed to the door to the left. "The dining room is through there."

"Thanks." She retreated from the kitchen, leaving Maverick with a burning question.

Would Dr. Patch give her good news or bad?

"What do you mean you can't tell me?" Violet plunked into a dining room chair and massaged her tensed neck muscles.

Dr. Martin was right. Dr. Opal Patch would indeed be hard to work with.

"I spoke to the medical examiner and Dr. Welborn agrees. We'll only discuss the case with the police. You're not the police."

Violet tightened her grip on her cell phone and resisted the urge to fling it across the room. While she realized Dr. Patch had every right not to discuss her findings, she wanted to be kept updated. She had a deep desire to give the Hancock family—namely Julia Hancock's sister, Heather Kane—closure. Two years had been too long for Heather to wait. Heather had pleaded with the public to help the police with any tips on the whereabouts of her niece, Amy. So far, no new leads had materialized.

"Can you at least tell me if Dr. Welborn determined the identity of the skull?"

"Too early. You should know that. You can get your updates from the police. Good night and stop bothering me." She ended the call.

Violet again resisted the urge to throw her phone. If only she had Dr. Martin's approval of her working the case on a recording. But in the heat of that dangerous moment and his death, she hadn't thought she'd need it.

She tucked her phone into her pocket and reentered the kitchen.

A white-haired man who reminded Violet of Santa stood beside Maverick. They both turned at her approach.

"Violet, this is Buck Lawson, the owner of Hawkweed River Ranch," Maverick said.

The man thrust his hand out. "Hey, little lady. So nice to meet you. Sorry for all your troubles."

She returned the handshake and quelled the chuckle bubbling inside. *He even sounds like Santa.* "Thank you for letting me stay here at the ranch. I didn't mean to bring my burdens to you."

"We're all God's creatures and I'm happy to help. I was just telling Maverick here that the ranch hands are aware of the situation and they will keep a close eye on the property. You're safe here."

Was she? After today, she wasn't so sure.

"I appreciate that, thank you. Your ranch is beautiful." Violet scanned the rustic kitchen. "I love all the log features."

Buck gestured toward Maverick. "It will be his and Austin's soon. Time for this old geezer to retire. I'm moving back to New Brunswick in January to live with my brother."

"I'll give you the tour tomorrow," Maverick said. "It's getting late. You've been through a lot today and you need rest."

She yawned as if on cue. "True."

"What did Dr. Patch say?"

"That she can't tell me anything." Violet clenched her jaw, reliving the conversation with the anthropologist. "I guess Colby was right about her. She won't be easy to work with. At least I know she's working on it."

"Maybe Mayor Coble can help with that."

"True. His daughter was close friends with Amy and is struggling." Violet checked her watch. "It's now eleven, so I'll call my supervisor tomorrow."

Wolf strutted over to Violet and nudged her leg.

Maverick laughed. "He likes you. He doesn't warm up to just anyone."

Violet bent over and kissed the dog's forehead. "Hey, Wolf. Thank you for protecting me today."

Woof!

She straightened. "I'm heading to bed. Thanks again, Buck."

"You're welcome, purty lady." He winked and hobbled from the room.

"He seems like quite the character. Reminds me of Santa."

"He's been told that several times. Buck is awesome and has taken me under his wing to bring me up to speed on his ranch." Maverick snapped his fingers. "That reminds me, Austin is coming and bringing his wife. She's a constable, so it will be good to have her here, too."

"Looking forward to meeting them." Violet yawned again. "I really need to get to bed. Night."

"See you in the morning. Sleep well."

She prayed that would be the case. Violet made her way up the spiral steps and down the hall. She tiptoed into Riley's room.

Marmalade raised her head from her position on the pillow beside the five-year-old redhead.

"Stay there, Marmy," Violet whispered. She blew her cat a kiss and backed out, then entered her guest room.

After changing into her flannel, green-and-red pajamas, Violet nestled under the buffalo plaid comforter and texted Sara.

How are you?

Bouncing dots displayed on her screen.

Good. You?

Tired. Dr. Patch isn't being helpful. Need the mayor to intervene.

More bouncing dots.

Want me to threaten jail time?

Violet added a laughing emoji. She loved this woman and her sense of humor. They had met at church when practicing for a Christmas pageant. They both sang in the choir and hit it off instantly.

Calling my supervisor tomorrow to put pressure on Dr. Patch.

A reply came instantly.

Good. Sleep well.

You too.

Violet hovered her finger over her mother's contact name. She needed to hear her voice, but at the same time, didn't want to talk to her. *Mom, why didn't you tell me about my sister? Ugh!* She realized her mother had her reasons, but Violet had a right to know.

She tossed her cell phone on the nightstand. She couldn't deal with Erica Hoyt right now.

Violet reached over to turn off the light as another text dinged on her cell phone. "What did you forget, Sara?"

She read the message.

Return what's mine, or else you die. You can run, but you can't hide forever. I have spies everywhere. R

Violet's chest tightened.

Ragnovica was now threatening her, too. Santa Man was right. Violet was definitely on this person's radar.

And now she'd never get to sleep.

SIX

The scent of freshly brewed coffee lured Violet into the kitchen after a few hours of restless sleep. She was normally a decaf drinker, but today she required an extra shot of caffeine if she was going to make it through the day. She entered the dimly lit room and walked to the window above the sink, peering out into the back of the property. Darkness still covered the area, but the light over the barn illuminated the heavy snow still blanketing the region. She sighed. She'd never be able to search for Amy in this weather.

"Morning, little lady," Buck said.

Violet's hand flew to her heart. "You scared me. I didn't see you sitting in the dark."

"This is my favorite part of my day. It's so peaceful and makes me wonder if this is how Mary and Joseph felt when Jesus was born, especially after their taxing journey to Bethlehem. Quiet. Joyful. Tranquil."

"I love this time of year."

The man's eyes burrowed into hers. "I can see you're tired. Even in the darkness. Help yourself to an espresso. Something tells me you need it."

"I didn't sleep well. Not because of the bed, just a haunting text that came in right before I turned out the light." Violet made her way to the machine and added a mug under the spout before hitting the correct brew option. "Tossed and turned all night."

"Cream is in the fridge."

"I'm good, thanks." She waited for the drip to finish and took her mug over to the table. "How long have you lived here?" She wanted to change the subject.

"Fifty years. Was born and raised in Moncton, New Brunswick. Moved to Alberta after high school to take a job on a ranch. Met my wife here, too." He pushed his finished coffee cup to the side. "I hear you're from a large family."

"Sure am. Seven kids." She slouched in her chair, her shoulders drooping. "Actually, that's not entirely correct. I just found out I have a twin that my parents never told me about."

He whistled. "That must have been a surprise."

"Yes. Apparently, the doctor told Mom that my sister Baylee died, but I believe after yesterday's events, that isn't the case." She took a sip of espresso. "I want to do a social media hunt for her today while I wait out this storm."

"Why would the doctors tell your mom she died?"

"The only thing I can come up with is an illegal adoption ring. My assailant called me by her name yesterday. Baylee Peck. You heard of her?"

"'Fraid not. She from around here?"

"No idea. We were born near Banff, but I'm thinking she must have recently been in the area." She ran her finger along her mug's rim. "I hate that Mom didn't tell me."

"I'm sure she had her reasons." Buck reached across the table and squeezed her hand. "God doesn't make mistakes, and He has a plan for all of this."

She jerked her hand away. "Lately, I've been doubting Him, so I'm having a hard time believing that."

"Doubts are only natural and God understands."

Violet studied the older man's bearded, kind face. "Thank you for saying that. Lately, when I've talked to Mom, she hasn't been as understanding. She's frustrated with me."

"Mamas have a way of doing that."

Marmalade trotted into the kitchen and hopped onto Violet's lap. "Morning, Marmy." She smiled at Buck. "Thank you for letting me bring my cat. I couldn't bear to leave her alone."

"She's a cutie."

Clicking claws on the hardwood announced Wolf's presence, followed by a bark.

Marmalade hissed and scattered off Violet, racing out of the room. No doubt in a hunt for a good hiding place.

"Sorry. Wolf gets too excited sometimes." Maverick made his way over to the counter. "I definitely need an espresso this morning. Vi, how did you sleep?"

"Not good."

Buck stood and took his mug to the sink. "You both need a good, ole-fashioned cowboy breakfast. Steak and eggs."

Violet laughed. "Not what I normally eat for breakfast, but I'll take it. Didn't eat much yesterday, so I'm hungry."

An hour later, Violet sat in the dining room with her laptop and her third cup of coffee, although she had switched to decaf after her espresso. Maverick and Wolf had gone outside with Buck to assess the snow situation.

Violet hit Kevin McGregor's number on her cell phone and waited.

"Morning, Violet. What news do you have?"

She updated him on yesterday's events and the text she'd received last night, including her conversation with Dr. Patch.

The man mumbled a few choice words. "That woman is insufferable. I've had to deal with her frequently when Dr. Martin wasn't available. Don't you worry. I will take care of this."

Did he miss the part about Ragnovica texting her?

"Thank you, sir. I know we haven't found Amy yet, but this storm has delayed our search."

"Well, right now you need to stay put, especially since Ragnovica has contacted you directly. I don't like it. Maybe Jill should take over."

"No. I can handle it."

"I'll request Constables Daley and Everett come and get your phone. Perhaps their digital forensics can find something that could help." A pause. "And before you say anything, I'll get you a new phone."

She let out a long breath. "Thank you, sir."

"I need you back out there once the storm passes. The mayor has been calling twice a day for updates."

"Understood. If Amy is in the park, Wolf will find her. He's good." She could no longer deny that fact after the dog's discoveries yesterday.

"I'll be in touch. Stay safe and don't go anywhere alone." He hung up without waiting for a reply.

The gruff older man could be abrupt, but he also had heart and looked after his employees.

Violet opened her laptop, bringing it to life. Time to search for her long-lost sister.

The front door opened and closed, followed by footsteps stomping down the foyer.

Maverick dashed into the room.

Wolf trotted behind him.

"Violet, one of the ranch hands has met Baylee. He's on his way here now."

Violet shot to her feet and swayed. She gripped the back of the chair to steady herself.

Was she closer to finding out the truth about her twin?

Maverick grabbed Violet around the waist to prevent her from collapsing. "Whoa. I've got you." He guided her back to the chair and tried hard to ignore her vanilla scent. Maverick remembered the aroma from their university days. He'd loved it back then and still did. *Not the time, Mav, to be thinking of Violet as more than a friend. She needs you to be a protector. Nothing else.*

And Maverick intended to right his wrong from all those years ago. He wouldn't fail her again.

Violet sat. "Tell me. Who met my sister?"

Maverick dragged out the chair beside her and plunked down. "One of the ranch hands, Gavin. He's on his way here. He recognized her name when I was talking to him. Says he went to high school with a Baylee Peck, but that was in British Columbia, so he's not sure if she's the same person."

Violet's eyes brightened. "But it's a start."

The front door opened and closed. Seconds later, a man in his thirties entered the dining room and halted, his jaw dropping.

"Gavin, do you recognize this woman?" Maverick pointed to Violet.

"It's been years, but yes, you must be Baylee's twin."

Violet stood. "Are you sure?"

He nodded. "Yes, I had a major crush on her throughout high school."

"But we all change. How can you be sure?" Maverick asked.

The man shoved his hands into his pockets, his shoulders slouching forward. "Because I kept tabs on her and creeped her social media pages."

"I need to look her up." Violet dropped into her chair and opened her laptop.

"Don't bother," Gavin said. "She took down all her profiles."

Violet's finger stilled on her touchpad. "Why would she do that?"

Gavin shrugged. "No idea."

"When was the last time you found her online?" Violet tapped on her laptop.

"About six months ago."

Violet's expression contorted. "You stalked her for all these years? Did you ever contact her?"

Maverick noted the alarm on Violet's face. "Gavin, do you know where she lives?"

He shook his head. "As I said, I lost track of her six months ago." He faltered for a second. "Wait, I distinctly remember her last post because it was odd."

Violet leaned forward. "Tell us. What did she say?"

"Something like, 'I found out their secret and they're gonna pay.' I thought it odd and when I checked her socials the next day to see if she posted an update, everything was gone."

Violet once again tapped on her laptop. "He's right. I can't find anything."

"It's like she disappeared."

"Did you ever contact her personally?" Maverick asked.

"Once, but she ordered me to stop harassing her." Gavin fiddled with the zipper on his winter jacket. "Not sure why, because I did nothing like that. I'm not that kind of person. Only wanted to say hi."

Maverick wanted to believe the man, but something about his demeanor sent both doubts and chills zinging through his body. "Anything else you can think of?"

The ranch hand gazed at the floor as if something had suddenly stolen his attention. "Nothing. I gotta get back to work clearing the snow." He left in a flash.

Violet got up and poured herself a glass of water. "Has Buck vetted all his employees?"

"I'm assuming so, but I'll check with him. Why do you ask?"

"He's hiding something. I don't buy his story. I can spot a stalker when I see one." She flattened her lips into an impregnable line.

Maverick analyzed her face. *There's a story behind her statement.* "Has someone stalked you, Vi? You can tell me."

She sipped her water as if gathering her thoughts.

Or was she simply stalling?

Why the secrets? *You should know. You didn't tell her everything about Piper.*

Violet finished her water and placed the glass in the sink. "I don't—"

Riley padded into the kitchen in her sock feet, rubbing her eyes and halting their conversation.

Maverick set aside his unanswered questions and approached his daughter. "Morning, Pumpkin. Did you sleep okay?"

She grunted at him and clamped her mouth shut.

Clearly ignoring her father.

Maverick's shoulders slumped. *Lord, how do I reach her? Help me.*

Riley spied Violet and raced to her side, hugging her leg. "Hi, Miss Vi."

Maverick couldn't read Violet's expression. Disgust? And was it directed at him?

She focused her attention on the five-year-old. "Did you like having Marmy sleep with you?"

Riley nodded.

"How about you let Daddy get you breakfast?"

She stomped and pouted. "No. You do it."

"Riley, Miss Vi is our guest. What if I make you chocolate chip pancakes?"

She crossed her arms. "Fine."

Was she five or fifteen? Her expressions not only reminded Maverick of a teenager, but of Piper. Her mother used to give Maverick that same expression whenever she didn't get her way. *Like mother, like daughter.*

"I can help." Violet's cell phone played Christmas bells, and she fished the device out of her pocket, glancing at the screen. "Dr. Patch. I need to take this. Somehow, I doubt it's good news."

"Understood."

Violet left the room.

Leaving Maverick with his five-year-old-turned-teenager.

He didn't know how to deal with her.

Lord, You put this little one in my life for a reason. Please show me how to reach her.

Maverick had fallen in love with Riley, but right now, he didn't need the additional worry in his life.

Not with a killer on the loose.

Violet braced herself for another tense conversation with the anthropologist and stepped into the foyer. She smiled, attempting to bring cheer into her voice. "Good morning, Dr. Patch."

She grunted. "Is it? I just got a disturbing phone call from our esteemed mayor."

So much for any cheer in their conversation.

"Ms. Hoyt, I don't appreciate being told what I can and can't do."

Violet steeled her shoulders as determination to stand her ground locked her muscles. "Dr. Patch, Dr. Martin was very clear that he wanted me to continue to be involved in this case."

"Why? You're only an archeologist."

Violet grimaced. How could she explain the desire to help the Hancock family? "Ever since I discovered the skulls, and we found out someone had not only murdered but buried the Hancock family in my park, I've felt a responsibility to find Amy and give her aunt closure." She had failed to keep her anger in check, but the woman infuriated Violet. Already.

She held her breath, waiting to hear how Dr. Patch would react.

"I know what you Hoyts are like. You can't always get your own way."

What? How did this woman know about her family? Then again, her father had been in the news multiple times over the past few years.

"Since the mayor threatened my job, I have no choice but to comply. Get to my lab now." She didn't wait for a response, but clicked off.

Violet checked her screen. "Goodbye to you, too." While she was glad the woman had invited her to the lab, Violet didn't like the thought of having to work with the cantankerous anthropologist.

God, why did you allow Dr. Martin to die? He was such a nice man.

Another question to add to her growing list for God.

Marmalade trotted down the steps and rubbed against her ankles, meowing.

Violet picked up her cat, cuddling her close. "At least I have you to brighten my foul mood."

The doorbell rang, startling Violet. Her cat scrambled from her arms.

Violet hurried to the door and opened it.

Sara stood on the step, frowning. "Why haven't you answered my calls?"

"What? You called? When?" Violet beckoned her inside out of the cold.

"Fifteen minutes ago."

Violet checked her phone log. "There's no record of your call."

Sara snatched the device. "That's it. You've had too many issues with this phone." She brought out another cell from her pocket. "Here's a new one, but only give your number to your family and anyone close to you." After a second, she added, "That you trust."

Laughter exploded from the kitchen. Seemed Riley's mood had shifted, but the question remained in Violet's mind. Would the girl warm up to her father?

"What are you doing today?" Sara's inquiry brought Violet's attention back to the constable.

"Heading to Dr. Patch's lab."

"No, you need to stay here. Santa Man just escaped custody and is threatening to find you."

What?

A shiver snaked up Violet's spine, settling around each vertebra and chilling her entire body.

SEVEN

Maverick finished updating Buck on the latest developments, requesting he tighten security with the news of the attacker's escape. Buck left to inform his employees. After Maverick had made Riley pancakes, she had warmed up to him a bit. Seemed chocolate was her favorite treat, and he even got her to laugh at one of his jokes. Right now, his daughter was in the kitchen baking cookies with the ranch's cook.

Violet sat in the living room rocker, biting her nails.

Her agitated state told him that the news of the escaped assailant had hit her hard.

Wolf sat beside her with his head resting on her lap. The K-9 sensed her panic and wanted to console his new friend.

Maverick approached Sara. "Do you have any idea where this man is? What happened? How did he escape custody?" He failed to contain his frustration, but Violet's life was at stake.

"Hold on. This isn't my fault." Sara looped her thumbs in her belt.

"Not saying it is, but how could he slip through your hands at the police station?" Maverick realized the two women were friends, but he had to ask the question.

"I wasn't on duty. Another constable was escorting him to jail, and he somehow got free of his cuffs." She turned to Violet and knelt in front of her. "He strangled the constable, causing an accident. Then he escaped."

Violet stopped biting her nails and took Sara's hands in hers. "This isn't your fault." She peeked around her at Maverick. "And you have no right to imply it was."

He slumped his shoulders. He couldn't win today. "I'm sorry. I didn't mean to suggest that."

Sara stood. "Listen, I know we're all on edge with yesterday's attacks, but let's work together."

"You're right. Violet's life is at stake. Did you ID Santa Man?"

The constable shook her head. "This is something I've only heard of happening on television, but he had burned off his prints."

Violet straightened in her chair. "What? Why would someone torture themselves by burning their fingers?"

"Agree. He wouldn't give his name, but he told us he's an operative for Ragnovica and was sent to take you out. Once he laid eyes on you, he couldn't do it. Apparently, even though this Baylee betrayed him, he still loves her."

Violet's mouth hung open.

"Unfortunately, our tiny station lacks the personnel to hold him and continue our other duties, so our sergeant ordered his transfer to Jasper." She checked her watch. "He escaped thirty minutes ago, so I rushed over here."

"Who all knows that Violet is at the ranch?" Maverick asked.

"Myself, Everett and our sergeant." She turned to Violet. "Unless you told someone."

"Only Supervisor McGregor." She placed her hands on her hips. "And I trust him."

"Good, then you're safe here and need to stay."

"I can't. I have to get to Dr. Patch's lab right away or she'll never involve me in her findings." Violet latched on to her friend's arm. "Please. Come with me."

Sara hesitated before releasing an elongated sigh. "I realize I can't convince you to stay put. Your Hoyt determination won't stop you, even when your life is at risk." She eyed Wolf, then turned her gaze to Maverick. "Can you come, too? I'd just feel better if she had Wolf and you by her side."

"Of course." Maverick looked out the front window. "How are the roads?"

"Plowed and getting better. The storm is subsiding. For now. They're calling for more, so if you have to go back into the park, we have to do it soon. They're saying we may get snowed in at Christmas."

"Let's go, then," Violet said. "I'll call my supervisor and Jill on the way. I have to give them my new phone number."

"And your family. I don't want the Hoyts on my back for not keeping them updated." Sara winked. "I'll inform my sergeant. Be ready to roll in five minutes."

"Wolf, come," Maverick commanded.

The dog hopped onto all fours, ready to work.

Thirty minutes later, after battling the roads, Wolf, Maverick, Sara and Violet entered the foyer of Asterbine Canyon Hospital where Dr. Patch worked.

Violet halted inside the revolving doors. "Let me handle this. Dr. Patch won't take kindly to the extra guests." She air-quoted *extra guests* and walked to the security guard sitting behind a desk. "We're here to see Dr. Opal Patch. She knows I'm coming. Violet Hoyt."

He pursed his lips and picked up the landline, punching in a number. "Dr. Patch. Violet Hoyt and company are here to see you." His eyes narrowed.

Evidently, the woman was giving him a hard time with Violet's company. Maverick braced himself for an argument.

And he would give one. He wasn't letting Violet out of his sight.

"Not sure, ma'am," the guard said. "Fine. I'll tell them." He slammed the receiver down and rolled his eyes before fumbling for badges. "That woman is unbearable. She didn't like that you brought other people, but agreed to let you in. Have fun. She's in one of her moods." He handed them badges and pointed to the right. "Elevators are that way. You'll need to scan your badge to get to her lab. It's on the lowest level."

"Bodies in the basement. How fitting." Maverick hung the badge around his neck.

The man snickered. "Just like in the movies. Nice dog, but she won't like it. She hates dogs."

"She has no choice. Wolf goes where we go." Maverick pointed to the dog's vest. "He's working."

"Understood." The guard tipped his head. "Have a good day."

The group made their way to the elevator, and Maverick scanned his badge and hit the button for the lower level. The elevator lurched before it descended.

Violet slumped against the wall. "I hate elevators."

"I remember that. You only took the stairs at our university. Don't worry, you'll be fine." Maverick moved beside her as if that would bring comfort.

A minute later, the elevator dinged and the doors opened.

They entered the chilled hallway and were greeted by the fortyish woman. Dr. Opal Patch leaned against the wall, scowling. "I didn't say you could bring all your friends, Ms. Hoyt."

"Let me handle this." Sara stormed around them and raised her badge. "Dr. Patch, Violet Hoyt is under both mine and this K-9 handler's protection."

Wolf barked.

Dr. Patch staggered backward.

Obviously, she not only didn't care for dogs, but feared them, too.

"Don't worry, Dr. Patch. Wolf won't hurt you." Maverick stalled for a split second. "Unless you provoke him or I order him to attack. I'm guessing there won't be a need for that, will there?"

The woman rolled her shoulders back and cleared her throat. "Just keep him on that leash." She held her left hand out. "This way." She mumbled under her breath and led them to the end of the corridor. She punched in a code and opened the door.

The group entered, and various scents assaulted Maverick's nose. Beside him, Wolf woofed. Not a bark or a growl, just him acknowledging that he smelled remains. Maverick petted his back. "Good boy."

"Is he okay?" Violet asked.

"He smells death. It's amplified in here." Maverick examined the lab. The large room held several tables with skeletal remains eerily arranged on them. The woman had her work cut out for her, especially now that Dr. Martin was gone.

"Which are the bones Wolf found?" Violet asked.

Dr. Patch approached the far table, stopped and gasped.

Maverick and Violet advanced farther into the lab.

Several bones lay on the floor, smashed into tiny pieces.

Someone had not only breached her lab, but tried to destroy the evidence.

This time, Wolf growled and barked.

A door slammed, echoing throughout the floor. The intruder was escaping.

Every muscle in Violet's body locked, sending her already frayed emotions into overdrive. Had Santa Man followed them to the lab? No, he couldn't have. Whoever had tampered with the evidence had already been here, just waiting to strike at the best opportunity. Which meant Dr. Patch was also in danger.

Or had she been the one who smashed the bones to throw them off track?

Sure, the woman was annoying, but would she do this?

Doubtful. She was known for being meticulous in her work and her pristine lab proved it. Skeletal remains lined in perfect order on the tables. Each separated exactly an inch a part. Everything was where it should be.

Except for the bones on the floor.

Sara's hand flew to her weapon. "Everyone, stay here and lock the door behind me. Maverick, Wolf needs to protect these ladies."

Maverick nodded and gave his K-9 the protect command. The dog's ears twitched, and he settled in between Violet and Dr. Patch.

Dr. Patch squirmed.

Violet leaned closer to the woman. "Don't worry. He won't hurt you. He's protecting us."

"I'm calling for backup." Sara spoke into her radio, updating Dispatch on the situation. She requested additional constables at Asterbine Canyon Hospital's lab. She withdrew her weapon and turned back to the group. "Stay here and don't open the door for anyone but me or my colleagues." She didn't wait for an answer, but raised her weapon and eased through the entrance.

Lord, keep her safe.

"Dr. Patch, isn't your lab locked?" Maverick asked. "You had to punch in a code to enter the room."

"Yes."

Violet's alarm level spiked. Could the attacker be one of her colleagues? "Who all has the code and where is the rest of your team?"

"I gave them this morning off as we worked late into the night. Only my team and the chief medical examiner, Dr. Welborn, have the code. And hospital security."

Violet studied the woman's tortured face. The breach and violation of her lab had clearly spooked the normally brazen anthropologist.

"Has Dr. Welborn been here?" Maverick moved closer to the door.

"Briefly last night, but she wanted me to finish my assessment before chiming in."

Violet squatted by the shattered bones, examining the pile. "It looks like they took a hammer to these. Dr. Patch, weren't you in here moments ago? Before we arrived?"

She shook her head. "I was doing paperwork in my office down the hall. This room is soundproof, so I heard nothing."

Violet placed her hands on her knees and pushed herself back into a standing position. She did a one-eighty, searching the room. "Where are the cameras, Dr. Patch? I know Dr. Martin had some installed last year."

Dr. Patch huffed and put her hands on her hips. "I had them

taken out yesterday. I don't like anyone spying on me while I work. Gives me the heebie-jeebies. Since I'm now the lead anthropologist for this part of Alberta, I requested they be taken out."

Violet withheld the remark that rose to her lips. That the woman had no right to do that so quickly after Dr. Martin's passing. Instead, Violet counted to five slowly. "Maverick, we need to get Sara to check the video footage in the hallway." She turned back to Dr. Patch. "Or did you have those removed, too?"

"Tried, but security vetoed that."

Honestly. The woman had nerve.

No wonder Dr. Martin warned me.

Violet's phone buzzed in her pocket. She bottled her irritation toward Dr. Patch and checked her cell phone's screen. Jill. She'd given her, Supervisor McGregor and her family the new phone number.

Went to your condo but noticed crews were fixing your door. They said no one was home. Where are you?

Violet flinched. How much should she tell her coworker? And was the timing of her text only a coincidence? Jill had never given Violet any reason to doubt her, but Sara told her to keep the fact that she was hiding at the ranch from everyone, including Jill. She tapped in a message.

At Dr. Patch's lab.

Dots bounced on the screen.

That woman is mean. Find anything out?

Jill had pegged Dr. Patch appropriately.

Not yet, but the bones were smashed.

A reply came instantly.

WHAT?

Yes, police investigating.

More bouncing dots.

Are we heading to the park?

Were they? The snow would definitely hamper their search, but from what Violet understood, Wolf could still uncover remains in the snow. After all, dogs could find avalanche victims.

I'll keep you updated. Stay tuned.

K

She pocketed her cell phone.

"Everything okay?" Maverick asked.

"Just Jill wanting an update." Violet positioned herself at the door and leaned in, listening for movement.

All was silent.

"Where is Sara?" She placed her hand on the doorknob.

Maverick pulled her back. "She said to stay here."

Right.

But Violet had a hard time waiting. It was something her mother always called her out on. "Fine. Dr. Patch, what information did you want to tell me?"

The woman looked up from studying the broken pieces. "Huh?"

"Why did you call me here?"

Dr. Patch had been acting strangely ever since they arrived, sending suspicion racing through Violet's mind. But then again, someone had violated her lab. Right?

She stood. "Couple things. My team and I examined these skeletal remains closely, specifically where they were severed. We then compared our findings with those of the skulls. They're consistent with the same crude marks and therefore we concluded they are the rest of the Hancock remains."

Violet's shoulders dropped, sorrow for what the family must have gone through setting in. How could anyone be so ruthless? "Any idea of the type of instrument used?"

"I hate to guess, but probably some type of handsaw."

"Wait, didn't Dr. Martin conclude that the family was shot? Wasn't there evidence of a gunshot wound on the forehead?"

"Yes, and it's my conclusion the heads were severed after death, but Dr. Welborn will say for sure." She motioned toward the pieces. "But that may prove difficult now."

"And was probably why the intruder did what they did." Violet scanned the rest of the tables. "Wait, where's the skull we found yesterday?"

"What the what?" Dr. Patch pointed to an empty lab table. "It was there."

Maverick walked to the area in question. "The intruder stole it? Why?"

"My guess is they didn't want us to figure out who it was." Violet's new cell phone dinged a news alert. She fished it out and tapped on the screen. "Great. That reporter Remi just posted an update to the Hancock family mystery. Now everyone is going to know. She cited us in her article." She raised her phone. "There's even a video." She hit Play.

Maverick and Violet stood by the skeletal remains as Remi tried to interview them.

Wolf stepped in front and barked, snarling his teeth.

The scene switched to Remi standing close to the yellow caution tape by the original burial site. "And folks, there you have it. Park archeologist Violet Hoyt is refusing to share information on this find, which leads this reporter to believe that it has something to do with the missing Hancock family. I've also ascertained that the dog you saw moments ago found more remains."

The camera spanned the area before returning to Remi.

"Two questions come to mind. Why would Ms. Hoyt not want to give Julia Hancock's sister closure, especially at this Christmas season?" She paused, obviously for effect. "And have they found little Amy Hancock yet? Be assured citizens of Asterbine Canyon, this reporter won't stop until she has answers. You all deserve that much. Until then, this is Remi Meyer, reporting from Asterbine National Park."

The video ended.

Maverick raked his fingers through his hair. "That woman has nerve accusing you of refusing to give information."

Violet bit the inside of her mouth, curbing her frustration. "She's always had it out for me." She dipped her head toward the Belgian Malinois. "I'm concerned she's now marked Wolf as a target."

Dr. Patch scowled. "I don't like how you're accusing her. The woman has been nothing but kind to me."

Figures.

A knock sounded. "It's me, Sara."

Violet thrust open the door. "Did you find the intruder?"

Sara and her partner, Nick, entered. "No, but additional officers are scouring the perimeter. Forensics are on their way."

"Great, more people in my lab." Dr. Patch's tone revealed her disgust. She flicked her fingers toward the door. "Ms. Hoyt, I have nothing else. You can leave now and take that beast with you."

Wolf growled.

"You hurt his feelings," Maverick said.

"Impossible. Dogs can't understand what humans say."

Wolf growled.

Maverick harrumphed. "Don't be so sure."

Sara raised her hands. "That's enough. Constable Everett is going to stay here and speak with the forensics team." She fished out Violet's bagged cell phone from her pocket and passed it to Nick. "I almost forgot. Give this to them. Have digital forensics check it for spyware." She addressed Violet and Maverick. "Time to go."

Violet zipped up her coat. "One thing you should also know is the intruder stole the skull." She pointed to the empty table. "Constable Everett, they need to concentrate on fingerprints there."

He dipped his chin in acknowledgement.

"Let's go." Sara opened the door.

The group followed and entered the elevator.

Violet punched the main floor button. "That woman grates on my nerves."

The elevator ascended.

"I think she does on everyone's," Sara said. "Did she—"

The elevator lurched upward, bypassing the main floor level, then screeched to a stop at the third floor.

Wolf barked.

Violet sucked in a breath. What—

An explosion rocked the car before they dropped.

The group yelled and sank to the floor as the elevator plummeted.

Maverick caught Violet's hand.

She clung tightly as her heart rate soared and spots flickered in her vision.

Had Ragnovica been watching them all along?

EIGHT

Maverick held Violet tightly with one hand and Wolf with the other. *Lord, please save us.*

Sara crawled to the panel and hit the emergency call button, holding it for a few seconds before yelling into her radio requesting assistance.

Would her cry be heard and help arrive to save them from whatever was about to happen?

Maverick watched as the floor numbers descended quickly. Seconds after they passed the main floor level, the car bounced to a stop.

"The emergency brakes kicked in." Sara stood and hit her radio button again. "Everett, the elevator stopped in between the first and lower level."

"I'm here. Constable Tucker and I are prying open the doors."

Scraping sounded below.

Seconds later, Sara's radio squawked. "Daley, the car is closer to the main level. We're headed there now. Hang tight."

"Bad choice of words, Everett," Sara replied.

"Sorry. Can you pry open the doors from the inside?" Nick's breathy reply indicated he was running.

"Maybe since it's an older building." Sara moved closer.

Maverick approached. "I'll help."

Together, Maverick and Sara jimmied the doors open, revealing Nick's observation. They were stuck in between the two floors.

Sara spoke into her radio. "They're open now."

"Good, security is here with the drop key. Are you all okay?"

Sara's eyes traveled from Maverick to Violet. "You good?"

They nodded. Maverick analyzed Violet's tortured expression and remembered she hated elevators. Her clouded eyes told him she was far from fine.

He eased himself down beside her. "Are you sure?"

She drew her legs up and rested her forehead against her knees. "I will be better once we get out."

"Everett, we're good, but hurry," Sara said.

The door above them opened, and the constable's face appeared through the opening. "We're assessing the situation."

A light shone upward before mumbles sounded between the constables.

"Daley, this isn't good. Tucker found explosives. We need to get you out. Now."

Maverick cringed as a movie flashed through his head. He prayed their situation wouldn't end in the same way. He had to get them all out now. "Violet, time to escape this tin can." He helped her stand.

"How?" She shuffled forward.

Sara turned from her position. "We have to climb."

Alarm registered on Violet's twisted face.

Maverick squeezed her shoulder. "I'll help you."

"And Everett will pull you through the hole." Sara gazed into the opening between floors. "It's wide enough for all of us to fit. One at a time. Vi, you've got this."

She bit her lip, but nodded.

Maverick positioned himself to her right. He intertwined his fingers together. "Step into my hands and I'll lift you up. Nick will grab you under the shoulders."

"You ready?" Sara yelled into the hole.

Nick reached his arms through. "Yes. Quickly."

Violet placed her palms on Maverick's shoulders and stuck her right foot into his hands.

"On three." Maverick mustered strength. "One. Two. Three."

She reached for Nick as Maverick thrust her upward. The constable hauled her through the opening.

One down. Three more.

Maverick focused on his dog. "Wolf, ready."

The Malinois barked.

"Wait, how are you going to get Wolf up there?" Sara asked.

Maverick unhooked his dog's leash. "Don't worry. He can jump high. This is nothing for him. Nick, move a bit to give him room."

The constable complied.

Maverick snapped his fingers and pointed toward Nick. "Wolf, up!"

The Malinois backed up slightly and ran, leaping in the air and up onto the floor. He skidded to a stop and turned toward the group, barking.

"Good boy." Maverick turned to Sara. "You're next." Once again, he cupped his hands. "Ready?"

"How will you get out?"

"Don't worry about me. Go."

She repeated the same process as Violet and Nick helped her through the hole.

"Your turn, Mav." Violet peered through the opening. "We've got you."

She didn't have to tell him twice.

Maverick backed up and—

The elevator dropped an inch.

He drew in a ragged breath.

"Maverick!" Violet's cry echoed throughout the shaft.

"Come on, buddy," Nick said. "Before it drops again."

Help me, Lord. Maverick squatted before thrusting himself upward, but missed the ledge and fell back into the elevator.

The group inhaled sharp breaths.

Come on, Mav, you've got this.

He held his breath, mustered strength into his limbs and leaped upward. His fingers caught hold of the ledge, but slipped.

The constables grasped Maverick's wrists and hoisted him through the hole.

Seconds before the entire elevator plunged downward.

A deafening crash echoed throughout the shaft.

Maverick's chest tightened as the realization that they all could have plummeted with the elevator settled into his weary muscles. *Thank You, Lord.*

Violet flew into his arms. "That was too close."

He held her tight, enjoying the feel of her in his embrace. "So glad you're okay."

Woof!

Maverick released his hold on Violet and dropped beside his dog, hugging him. "Yes, you, too. Good boy."

Wolf nestled into Maverick.

"Constable Tucker, you saw the explosives?" Sara asked.

Maverick reattached Wolf's leash and stood, eyeing the younger officer.

"I did. What was left of them. My dad was in the bomb unit, so he taught me what to look for." Tucker pointed to Wolf. "That dog is impressive."

"He sure is." Maverick observed the crowd that had formed in the lower lobby, and he contemplated whether criminals returned to the scene of their crimes, as was usually believed. "Could the perp be watching us?"

"Possible, but I have a feeling whoever did this is long gone." Nick unhooked his radio from his shoulder. "Now that you're all safe, we'll be questioning everyone. Someone may have seen something. I'll get constables to check the perimeter." He spoke into the mouthpiece and instructed the constables to search the building and grounds for not only the perp, but any explosives.

Sara leaned into Violet. "It's clear to me that someone is indeed watching and targeting you. We need to get you back to your location. Stat."

"Agreed," Nick said. "I'll get security to evacuate the rest of the building. Just in case."

"I'll reconnect with you later." Sara nudged Violet toward the entrance with one hand secure around her friend's arm and the other resting on the Glock at her waist.

Sara stopped and hit her radio button. "Is the front clear, Constable Tucker?"

"Affirmative," he replied.

The group exited and headed toward Sara's cruiser.

Sara stopped in her tracks. "Hold up."

Maverick followed the trajectory of what held her attention.

A paper secured under the windshield wiper flapped in the wind.

She lifted it with her gloved hand.

They read over her shoulder.

See how close I can get to you all. This was a warning. Vi, stay out of the park or you and your friends die.

Violet fell to the ground. "No!"

Wolf suddenly lifted his nose and barked nonstop.

"What is it, boy?" Maverick squatted in front of his dog.

The K-9 continued to bark.

Whatever it was, Maverick had to release his dog. He unhooked his leash.

Wolf hopped onto the parking lot's cement posts and barreled across the top of each, his focus clear. Catch the person responsible.

And the Malinois had caught the scent of the assailant.

Violet blasted to her feet and watched as Wolf did the unthinkable. Raced across the tops of the posts. "How does he do that?"

"He's incredibly strong and has high energy." Maverick turned to Sara. "He smells something."

"Does he normally do that without you giving a command?" she asked.

"Not always, but he sensed our heightened anxiety. I need to follow him. Violet, stay with Sara." Maverick sprinted after his dog.

"Not a chance." Violet followed.

Sara yelled into her radio, intent on protecting her friend and catching whoever Wolf was after.

In the distance, Wolf reached the end of the lot and hopped down from the post before rounding the corner of the building.

People observed the dog from their cars, their jaws hanging open. Obviously, they too were amazed at the K-9's abilities.

Violet returned her attention to the task at hand and followed Maverick around the corner.

Wolf's barking increased.

A masked individual with a Santa hat on, carrying a backpack, turned at the dog's presence.

A van stopped in front of the man, and the side door rolled open.

Wolf reached the assailant and tugged at the suspect's coat.

The individual wiggled out of his parka, dropped the bag and hopped into the van. The vehicle's tires spun on the snow-covered ice and swerved before the van shot out of the side parking lot.

Sara darted after it, yelling the plate number into her radio.

Wolf sat beside the bag and barked, placing his paw on top.

Maverick turned. "He's alerting to something in that bag. That's why he took off."

Sara jogged to their location. "What is he barking at?"

Violet pointed to the backpack.

Sara unzipped the top and staggered backward.

Violet inched closer to discover the cause of her friend's reaction.

The stolen head.

The reason the assailant had attacked them.

They wanted this woman's identity to remain hidden. Why? Would it expose them?

An hour after returning the skeletal remains to Dr. Patch, Violet entered the living room at Hawkweed River Ranch. Sara had ensured they weren't being followed by taking multiple back roads to the ranch. She vowed to keep them updated on the investigation. Dr. Patch too had promised to provide her findings after she conferred with Dr. Welborn.

Whimpering sounded from the room's corner, but Violet failed to see anyone nearby. She followed the cries and discovered Riley hiding behind the couch, crying, holding Marmalade.

Violet approached cautiously. "Honey, what's wrong?"

Two big blue eyes peered up at her, and fat tears rolled down the five-year-old's cheeks. "I want my mama."

Violet's heart melted at the sorrow the little girl was going through. "Bring Marmy and come sit with me, okay?"

Riley sniffed and nodded, shimmying out from her hiding spot with Marmalade in tow. Then she plunked down on the couch.

Violet brought her and the cat into an embrace. "It's gonna be okay. I know you miss your mom. But I'm glad your daddy is here. Do you want me to go get him?"

The child stiffened in Violet's arms and recoiled. "No! I hate him."

Marmalade squirmed from Riley's sudden tantrum and fled off the couch.

Irritation toward Maverick tightened Violet's muscles. What had he done to make Riley speak the angry words?

Not that Violet had any experience with parenthood, but perhaps a woman's perspective would help. "Let's just us girls talk. Okay?"

Riley sniffed again and wiped her nose with the back of her hand. "K."

Violet struggled for words but wanted to help. Tragic events had uprooted the little girl's life and torn her mother away.

"Tell me. Do you like Christmas?"

Riley's eyes brightened. "Yes." Then her eyes clouded. "But will Santa find me this year?"

"Of course. Don't you worry your pretty little head about that." She tapped on Riley's nose.

She giggled.

"Honey, why don't you like your daddy?"

Her lip quivered. "Mama told me Daddy hated me. That's why he never came to visit."

Violet flinched. Was that true? It didn't add up to what Maverick had told her. She had seen his gentleness toward Riley but had he left something out of his story? Why would a mother lie to her daughter?

Violet let out a small cry at that question. Her own mother had kept her twin a secret but claimed it was so she wouldn't suffer. Could that be the same reason Piper had fibbed?

But still. To tell someone their father hated them seemed harsh for a mother to say to her five-year-old daughter.

A branch slapped the window, bringing an idea to Violet's mind. She turned to Riley. "Do you know what a snow angel is?"

She hopped down from the couch. "Yes. Can we make some?"

The image of the escaped Santa Man came to mind. Surely they'd be safe if they stuck close to the house. Besides, there were lots of protectors on the property.

Violet stood and reached for the girl's hand. "Let's go."

After bundling Riley and herself up, Violet picked a spot beside a spruce tree in the front yard. "This looks like a great place to make angels. Come on."

They plunked down onto the snow and lay back. Violet turned her head to face Riley. "Ready?"

She nodded.

"Go." Violet spread her arms out and moved them up and down, creating the wings. "Done."

They stood and admired their creations.

Violet's wings smothered Riley's little ones.

Riley clapped. "That was fun. Let's do another!"

Wolf barked.

Violet turned toward the sound. Maverick and Wolf approached.

"Wolfy, come see me," Riley yelled.

The dog glanced at his handler as if asking for permission.

"Wolf, go," Maverick commanded.

The dog tumbled through the snow and reached Riley within seconds.

Riley hugged him. "I woof you."

The two frolicked, rolling around in the snow together.

"What are you two gals doing?" Maverick eyed the wings. "Ah, snow angels."

"We were having some girl time." She analyzed Riley playing with Wolf. "He loves her."

"Yah, and she does him. Just wished she'd warm up to me, too."

Violet hesitated. Should she share what Riley had said? Perhaps he'd open up more. "Maverick, she told me that her mother said you hated her and didn't want to visit."

His eyes widened, then narrowed. "How could I hate someone I didn't realize existed?"

The anger in his voice drew Wolf's attention, and he scrambled up, shaking the snow from his fur.

Riley stared at her father, her lip protruding.

"I did it again. My harsh tone reared its ugly head. Vi, you know me. I would never do that to a child, especially my own."

Violet remembered his interaction with children when Angie's little sisters came for a visit. He had confessed to loving children, stating he wanted lots.

She grazed his arm. "You're right. Just give her time and show her acts of love. I don't mean Christmas presents either. Find out what she likes and shower her that way."

"Good advice." He stared at his child. "First, I need to tell her I'm glad she's here."

"Good idea."

Maverick squatted in the snow in front of his daughter. "Riley, Daddy needs to tell you something."

She looked up from petting Wolf. "What?"

"I'm glad you came to live with me, Pumpkin." He hugged his daughter. "I love you."

She kicked out of his hold. "No, you don't. I hate you." She ran across the lawn and up the steps, plunking herself in the large chair on the veranda.

Maverick stood and hung his head. "That went well."

"Give her time. Remember, acts of kindness." Violet's cell phone rang. She fished it from her pocket and looked at the screen. "It's Mom. I better take this."

"See you inside. I'm going to talk to Riley again."

"Go easy on her." Violet hit Answer and plodded through the snow toward the ranch. "Hey, Mom."

"Little lady, how are you?"

"I'm fine. What's up?" She hated to sound rude, but her mother was the last person she wanted to talk to right now. She was sad it had come to that, but Violet was finding it hard to forgive her.

"Other than that quick text after your break-in, I haven't heard from you. I just wanted to ensure you're safe."

Violet entered the ranch and stomped the snow from her boots. "Sorry, I should have called. I'm safe." Was she? Violet wasn't so sure after today's events.

"Where are you?"

Violet explained.

"I'm glad you're not alone." A pause. "Listen, there's another reason I called. I wanted to tell you I've told the rest of the family about your twin."

"How did they react?"

"Shocked. Hurt. Like you." Her voice quivered. "Your father and I thought what we were doing was the best for you. For our family."

Violet tightened her grip on the phone and plunked into a

nearby chair in the large foyer. "I realize that, Mom, but I deserved to know. We all did."

"You're right. Frank and I also contacted our local constable to question the doctor who told us she was dead. It's been years, but we wanted the police to put pressure on him."

"What did you find out?"

"He confessed to needing the money. Vi, your sister *is* alive."

Violet popped off the chair. "I have to find her." This confirmed Gavin's story. Baylee was alive. "Mom, she's in danger."

"I'm getting Constable Porter to contact the constables at Asterbine Canyon's police station to provide the information the doctor did. He knew little, but it may help with the investigation."

"Good idea."

"Knowing Baylee is alive is the best Christmas present a mother could ask for." The excitement in her mother's voice softened Violet's heart.

But also added to her angst. If Ragnovica found out that Violet wasn't Baylee, then the criminal boss would stop at nothing to silence both of them.

Violet didn't come this far to find her sister, only to lose her again.

NINE

Multiple dings exploded on Violet's phone, thrusting her out of a restless sleep and dreams of a masked Santa kidnapping Riley. She cried out and sat up in bed. She pressed her hand against her chest to still her racing heart. *Just a dream, Vi. Just a dream. Riley's okay. You're safe.* She breathed in and exhaled slowly. She had spent the rest of the day yesterday searching for some sign of Baylee on the internet, but Gavin was right. There was no record of her. Violet had requested Sara to contact Constable Porter of the Bowhead Springs Police Department to get what information he might uncover. There had to be some account of a Baylee Peck somewhere. Taxes. Social Insurance Number. Something.

Or had her parents erased her birth records? Was that even possible?

"Ugh!" Violet pounded the bed, disturbing her cat. Marmalade hopped down and scurried out of the room. "Get it together, girl."

She reached for her phone and unhooked the charger, swiping her thumb across the screen. Texts appeared from Jill asking when they were heading back into the park. Another from her supervisor reminding her he was counting on her to find Amy before Christmas. Violet's mother had also called three times.

Sara had left a text for Violet to call as soon as she got up. She had news.

Violet hit her friend's number and waited.

"Morning. How'd you sleep?"

"Not the best. What news do you have?" Violet winced. She

was impatient, and that wasn't the way to greet her best friend. "Sorry, I guess I woke up on the wrong side of the bed."

"Hey, I get it. Someone attacked you two days in a row. That would put anyone in a foul mood."

Violet flung her legs over the bed and stepped into her slippers, making her way to the window. "Yah, let's not make it a third. What's your news?"

"Constable Porter relayed information regarding his interview with the doctor who declared Baylee dead. Apparently, he had a gambling habit and needed the money."

Violet harrumphed. "Not a good reason. What else did he say?"

"Something interesting. Baylee wasn't the only baby he stole from their biological parents."

"Did he say where he took the babies?" Violet parted the window blinds to check the weather. The sun was shining. Good. Perhaps she could get some searching done.

"That's the interesting part. He said the person only contacted him through encrypted emails and he doesn't know their real name. They told him to take the babies to Asterbine Shipping Company."

Violet pivoted. "What?"

"Yes, they have a branch near Calgary. Constable Porter is heading there now to find out more information. I'm going to the one here in Asterbine. Dig for answers."

"That's good news."

"Hope so. Vi, I need you to stay at the ranch. Can you do that?"

"Sara, I have to work. Kevin says the mayor is hounding him. We need to find Amy. Her aunt deserves closure."

A sigh filtered through the phone. "I'll swing by after my visit. Wait for me."

"Fine. Any updates on the break-in at Dr. Patch's lab?"

"That's the other news I had. No prints, but we got a hit on the license plate number. Van is owned by—get this—Heather Kane."

Violet's jaw dropped. "What? That's Amy's aunt. Why would Heather try to steal the remains?"

"We haven't established it was her yet. Everett is going to see her today."

"Wow, you are a bundle of news this morning."

"Yup. Gotta run. Remember, you promised to stay at the ranch."

"Yes, Mom."

Sara chuckled and severed the call.

Ten minutes later, Violet sauntered into the kitchen and almost collided with Maverick. "Whoa. Sorry, didn't see you. You're up early."

"Couldn't sleep. Too much going through my brain." Maverick lifted a mug off the rack and poured himself a coffee. "Yum. Gingerbread flavor. Buck likes to change it up every day."

Violet followed suit, bypassing the espresso machine, and held her mug out. "Yes, please. That's one of my faves. When does Austin arrive?"

"Today sometime. He and Izzy are spending Christmas here and we're finalizing the deal on the ranch." He filled her mug.

Violet cupped her coffee in her hands, letting the heat warm her chilled body. "I'm sorry for intruding on your family time." She focused her attention on her mug.

"Don't be silly. Riley and I enjoy having you here." He lifted her chin. "I'm grateful that we've reconnected after all these years. I've missed our friendship."

She gazed into his sapphire-colored eyes. *I could get lost in those baby blues.* Old feelings for this man bull-rushed her. Friends? Did she suddenly want more? "Mav, I—"

He retreated, his face contorting.

No, he didn't feel the same. That was obvious in his shift of demeanor.

He opened the fridge and brought out cream. "Oh, I almost

forgot. Buck is having a Christmas party tonight. Ranch-style, in the barn. Apparently, he does it every year as his way of showing his staff how much he appreciates them. You're invited."

"I don't want to intrude."

"I won't hear any more of this you're intruding stuff. You deserve a little fun after a rough couple of days."

She smiled and sipped her coffee. "True. Riley will love that."

"I hope so."

"I almost forgot to tell you. Sara had lots of news for me today." She shared all the information her friend had given her, including her warning to stay at the ranch.

"That sounds promising. Maybe there's an end in sight and we'll be able to celebrate Christmas in peace. I need a win with Riley."

She scrutinized his handsome face. Something still bothered him. "Mav, you're holding details back on what happened with Piper. You can trust me. I may be able to help." Not that she was an expert on relationships. After all, hers ended up with the scar on her abdomen and her boyfriend in jail.

His eyes clouded, and he set his mug on the counter. "I need to feed Wolf and get to work. I'm looking into some puppies I want to bring to the ranch." He left.

She frowned. What was so terrible that he couldn't tell her?

Her cell phone dinged, and she dug it out of her jeans pocket, swiping the screen. An email from an address she didn't recognize. Spam or something else, but it was the subject line that caught her eye.

I know who you are.

Not being able to resist the temptation, she clicked and opened it.

Saw the news. You look like her. Here's a tip for you. Don't trust Remi Meyer. I'll be in touch.

The email included a link. Should Violet risk clicking on it? She realized how spammers worked, but this felt different. Important. Her instincts were telling her to proceed.

And she always listened to her gut, especially after Angie's death. The secret she held from Maverick about her friend's death still haunted her after all these years. Which was why she didn't blame him.

No, she blamed herself.

Not willing to make that mistake again, she clicked the link.

Remi appeared onto her screen. It was dark, and she was talking to someone standing in the shadows. "I can't do that. That will expose everything I've worked so hard to get. They buried her with it. We have to go back. It's my story and no one else's."

A mumbled reply came. The only word Violet could make out was "Baylee."

Violet sucked in a breath. What was this reporter up to and did she know her sister?

She leaned closer to get a better look at the person she was talking to, but they remained hidden in the shadows, as if they realized they were being filmed.

Ragnovica?

Whoever it was, Violet had to send this video to Sara and get her to question the reporter.

She hit Forward and tapped in a message before sending it to Sara.

Another email blasted into her inbox. From the same, unknown email address. The subject line caught her attention.

Go to the park. Now.

She opened the message.

Violet, I know you opened my email. I'm not the enemy and you can trust me. Go to the park where you found that woman's head. They are going to dig up the rest of her remains. Find them first. A key piece of evidence was buried with her.

What? *Who is this person?*
Violet hit Reply and tapped in a message.

Who are you, and how do I know this isn't a trap?

She realized she shouldn't reply and forward the email to Sara, but the urgency demanded her immediate attention. Ignoring her tingling Spidey senses, she hit Send.

And waited.

Seconds later, another email dinged with one sentence that sent her heartbeat skyrocketing.

Because I'm your sister.

Violet couldn't silence her sharp inhale. Her sister had found her, and right now Violet had to comply.

Time was running out.

"Are you sure this is a good idea?" Maverick drove into the Asterbine National Park's lot. "Didn't Sara tell you to stay at the ranch?"

Violet flinched. "Yes, but that was before my sister emailed me."

She had shared with him the emails and the video that exposed Remi. "And you're convinced it's really Baylee? Seems like a coincidence. This could be a trap."

"I've texted Sara to tell her where we're going. Jill is also on her way." She motioned toward the K-9 cage in the back. "Besides, I have you and Wolf to protect me."

"So, we're going back to where we found the head? Wolf didn't alert to any other remains there."

"She said it was close, and we got interrupted by masked Santas and Remi."

"Yah, I knew something was off about her."

A vehicle drove into the lot and parked beside them.

Violet opened her door. "That's Jill. Let's go. We have to beat whoever else is on their way here." She climbed out of the SUV.

"Wait!" Ugh. Violet still had the same impatient streak he remembered from university. Maverick scrambled out of his vehicle and around to the back, hitting the button to open the hatch. He lifted the latch on the cage. "Wolf, come."

The dog hopped down. Maverick attached his leash, then brought out Buck's shotgun.

Even though he trusted Wolf with his life, Maverick wanted the added protection in their unwise adventure into the park.

He attached his backpack before approaching Violet and Jill.

Violet halted their conversation and pointed to the shotgun. "Why did you bring that?"

"Isn't it obvious? I'm not going into the wilderness again unarmed."

Her bottom lip quivered. "Get it away from me! I hate guns."

Hate them or scared of them?

Jill held out her hand. "Violet, this is a smart move. I'll take it, Maverick. You stay close to her with Wolf."

Maverick examined Violet's terrified expression before passing the shotgun to Jill. "Can you shoot?"

"Of course. My daddy taught me. We used to hunt deer together. What can I say? I was a bit of a tomboy." Jill put on her backpack containing her folded shovel and other archeological tools hanging from various loops before clutching the weapon. "I'll go ahead, but stay close." She set off toward the park's entrance.

"Violet, what's going on?"

She hooked her ground-penetrating device to her backpack. "Nothing. Just hate guns." She took off in the direction Jill had headed.

Maverick hissed out a breath and turned to his dog. "What's that all about?"

He barked.

"You're right. Let's go." Maverick gently jerked the leash. "Come."

The duo followed the stubborn woman into the wilderness.

Thirty minutes later, the group reached the site where they'd found the skull. The trek there had been difficult since the area was now covered in snow.

Violet examined the region, walking around and squatting now and then.

"What are you doing?" Maverick asked.

"Locating the exact spot where we found the head. The snow has covered everything." She pointed. "Wait, it was here."

"So, now what?" Jill shifted her hold of the shotgun.

Violet unhooked her GPR device and passed it to Jill. "You use this. Maverick, time to get Wolf searching."

"On it." Maverick unleashed his K-9. "Wolf, seek!"

The dog sniffed the area, raised his head and sprinted down a snow-covered path.

"Let's go." Maverick trudged through the snow in the same direction.

"Wait, I'll stay here and use the GPR." Jill pointed in the opposite direction from where Wolf had headed.

Maverick stopped and turned. "I trust my dog."

Violet drew her hat farther onto her head, glancing between her colleague and Maverick.

"Come on, Violet. You've seen what Wolf can do."

"He's right. You search here, Jill. You have your two-way?"

"Yes."

"Radio me if you find anything. Sara should be here soon, but stay safe." Violet joined Maverick at the trailhead. "Let's go."

They plodded through the trees, but Maverick had lost sight of his dog. "Wolf, speak!" The command he'd taught him to bark.

A bark sounded to their right. "That way."

Moments later, they found Wolf sitting beside a rock formation among a cluster of spruce trees.

"He's found something." Maverick rushed forward. "What is it, boy?"

The dog placed his paw on the middle rock and barked.

Maverick turned back to Violet. "There are remains here. Hand me your shovel and get Jill to our location."

Violet complied and radioed for Jill to come, giving her their position, then tapped a message to Sara on her cell phone.

On my way, Jill replied seconds later.

Maverick dropped beside Wolf. "We have to hurry."

Violet kneeled beside him and dug, using her gloved hands. "Be careful, though. We can't destroy evidence."

"And do all that before this Ragnovica comes." He guffawed. "No pressure."

"Right. I texted Sara our location. Just hope it went through. You never know in this park."

Fifteen minutes after clearing the snow, Maverick lifted the dislodged rock out of the way. "Where's Jill? She should have been here by now?"

"Good question." She pressed her radio button. "Jill, where are you?"

Silence answered.

Violet turned to him. "I don't like it."

"She may have had difficulties finding this spot." He peered into the hole they'd created. "What's that?"

Frayed fabric poked up from the soil.

Violet brought out her trowel and gently dug around the item, exposing the fabric nestled into the skeletal remains. "This is it. We found her."

"Something tells me these haven't been here for two years. Could this be a totally different person?"

"Hopefully, Dr. Patch and Dr. Welborn will answer that question."

The sun peeked through the trees, casting a ray of light into the shallow grave. An item sparkled and drew Maverick's attention. "There's something else here." He pointed.

Violet removed her brush and worked at clearing the soil. "It's a chain, but it's stuck on a root. Do you have a pocketknife?"

He fished one out of his pocket and handed it to her. She set her brush aside and pressed the button to release the blade, cutting the root. She stuffed the knife into her pocket and lifted the object in question, raising it in the air.

Maverick flinched. A pink heart dangled from the chain, but it was the line down the middle that drew his eye. "Wait, I've seen these before. Open the heart."

Violet pried the two halves apart and lifted one half. "It's a USB drive. This is what Baylee was talking about."

Maverick stood. "We need to get that to the police before—"

Wolf growled, then barked.

A shot rang out through the mountainous region.

It was too late. They'd found them.

TEN

Violet pivoted toward the direction of the shot and noted red in the trees. *Not Santa Man again.* She stuffed the necklace into her pocket, knowing it was probably the item they wanted. "We have to find Jill and get out of here."

"You're going to leave the remains behind?" Maverick clipped the leash back onto Wolf's collar.

She didn't want to, but knew it was only a matter of time before the assailants reached the site. After all, they'd buried the bodies, not realizing this person had the USB drive. "This is what Remi referred to in the video. Could it also be what Santa Man thought I had?"

"I'm guessing it is." He pointed to her radio. "We need to warn Jill."

Once again, Violet spoke into her two-way. "Jill, we found it. Where are you?" She waited. "Come on. Answer me."

Seconds later, a reply came. "I'm back at my truck. Need to get to the park station. Sorry. Couldn't answer you earlier. Thought I heard someone in the woods."

Maverick nudged her forward. "We have to move. Go."

Violet quickly covered the grave with snow, hoping to at least hide the remains from those lurking in the forest. She'd contact Dr. Patch to have her team extract them. Right now, she had more important things on her mind.

Get out of the forest and back to safety.

She put on her backpack and followed Maverick. "Jill, heading your way."

"Copy. Hurry."

A question lingered in her mind, and she hit her radio button again. "Why did you go back to the parking lot?"

"I had to—" A shot boomed through her radio.

"Jill!"

Silence.

Wolf barked.

Red flashed through the trees.

"Run, Vi!" Maverick dashed across the snow, holding on to his dog.

She followed.

A bullet lodged in the tree beside her.

She screamed and dropped into the snow. How she wished she hadn't demanded Maverick not carry the shotgun. As much as she hated guns, right now, they could use the added protection.

"Violet!" Maverick came to her side and helped her stand. "Stay low."

She turned to catch a glimpse of the shooter, but the figure had disappeared. "I think he's gone."

"Let's hope so. We need to get back to Jill."

Violet inspected the area, getting her bearings. "Wait, I know another way to the parking lot." She ducked under branches to her right and proceeded.

Once the trio made their way down the mountain, Violet's phone dinged with multiple texts.

Probably all from Sara.

She'd look at them later. Right now, she wanted to get to Jill.

Maverick stopped in front of her and held up his fisted right hand.

"What is it?"

"I see something ahead. You stay here." He passed her the leash. "Wolf, protect."

The Malinois inched closer to Violet.

"Where are you going?" she asked.

"Looks like someone is lying in the snow ahead, and I have

to check it out. Jill might be hurt." He raised his gloved index finger. "Don't argue. If this is a trap, I don't want you involved."

"But why isn't Wolf alerting to the danger?"

"Not sure. Stay here. I'll be right back." Maverick parted the branches and crept forward.

Violet peeked through but her view was obstructed by trees and snow.

Beside her, Wolf growled.

Violet held tightly to the K-9. "What is it, boy?"

Another shot rang out.

"Violet, run!" Maverick's frantic cry echoed through the trees, followed by deafening silence.

"Wolf, come." She remembered the command Maverick had given the dog multiple times. The duo followed the same route as Maverick.

There was no way she wouldn't help him.

They reached the lot where Maverick's SUV and Jill's truck were parked.

But both were nowhere to be seen.

"Maverick!" Violet did a one-eighty, searching for signs of them. "Jill!" *God, no. Please help them be okay.*

Wolf whimpered beside her.

She pivoted at the dog's cry, and gasped.

Maverick's hat lay next to a patch of blood.

Violet dropped to her knees. "No!" She had to find Maverick quickly. Was Jill with him?

Wolf poked his snout into her neck, reminding her of this dog's talents.

She stood quickly as an idea formed, but first she had to get the police to her location. Violet brought out her phone and called 911. "Please work."

The operator answered, asking how she could help. Violet identified herself and explained the situation, requesting assistance at her location.

"Emergency personnel are on their way. Stay there, Ms. Hoyt. Wait for them."

"Please tell them to hurry." Violet clicked off.

No way would she wait. She had a powerful weapon at her disposal. But how could she get Wolf to do what Maverick trained him to do? *Think, Vi.*

Violet rolled her shoulders, snatched the hat off the ground, and held it under the K-9's nose. *What was the command again?* "Wolf, seek!" Violet shouted the word *seek*, lacing it with authority.

The dog sniffed the hat, raised his nose in different directions before bolting to the left. He'd caught his handler's scent and was determined to save him.

Violet darted after Wolf and prayed for God's help, but would He listen?

Maverick's head throbbed, and he reached to silence the pounding but couldn't free his gloved hands. He jerked his eyes open. Where was he? What happened? The last he remembered was finding blood beside Jill's truck when movement sounded behind him. He had yelled to Violet to run before someone hit him over the head. He blinked his eyes to clear his foggy vision.

And drew in a sharp breath.

He was lying on the ground at the top of an icy, steep hill near a partially frozen lake. What was he doing here and who had abducted him?

Maverick tried to sit up, but his woozy head spun. He fell back and observed the area. Snow-covered trees surrounded the lake. A small dock was positioned to his left. Large rocks blanketed the shore—and he was dangerously close. One swift move and he'd tumble down the incline. He had to escape the icy hill.

"You weren't supposed to wake up." The voice came from behind.

"Who are you, and what do you want?"

The man stepped beside Maverick.

Santa Man without his hat or mask. Only the scars and tattoos displayed proudly—the escaped prisoner.

And somehow Maverick guessed he wouldn't make it out of the situation alive. *Lord, I need help right now. Send someone. Send Wolf.*

Wait, why hadn't Wolf alerted? "What did you do to my dog? Why didn't he catch your—" Maverick halted. What was that odor?

Peppermint oil. Had the man bathed in it?

"You rubbed oil on yourself. That can confuse dogs." Maverick held his breath to get a break from the potent scent.

"I've been researching. Can you tell?" The goon sneered. "But I left something behind when I took you. Something that will help Wolf find you."

Maverick's long bang rustled in the wind when he realized what the man was referring to.

Maverick's hat was gone.

"Why? Why do you want my dog to find me?"

"Because Ragnovica wants him dead. He's too good at his job and Ragnovica can't have him finding anyone else."

Maverick's pulse skyrocketed at the thought of someone harming his dog. *No, Lord. Don't let them kill Wolf.* "You mean Amy."

"I need what your girlfriend found."

The USB device.

Maverick pulled at his bound wrists. He had to break free and stop the man.

And save his dog.

Keep him talking. Find out as much as you can.

"I'm curious. What type of business is Ragnovica in?"

"None of your concern." The man mumbled under his breath.

"What's on the USB drive?" More importantly, was that the evidence Violet supposedly had?

"No idea. Just know that Ragnovica wants it, as it would destroy the empire." He leaned closer. "And the company will stop at nothing to silence anyone who stands in their way. Even that horrible dog."

Maverick attempted to free himself again, but his restraints wouldn't budge. Another question came to mind. "What is it of yours that you think Violet has? The flash drive?"

"No!" His eyes hardened, flashing venom. "You're gonna die in a few minutes. You're gonna tumble down that hill and you'll go through the ice because Wolf can't save you. He'll be dead."

Wolf's bark sounded in the distance.

A vise clamped around Maverick's heart, elevating his blood pressure. *No, Wolf, stay away!*

Santa Man snickered. "Good, he's coming."

He knelt beside Maverick.

"What are you doing?" Maverick failed to suppress the terror in his voice.

"Getting into position and waiting for the right timing." He laughed. "You lose. I win. Ragnovica will reward me for your death and the dog's."

Wolf's barking drew louder. He was almost there.

No!

Wolf bounded through the tree line, racing over the top of the rocks along the shoreline toward Maverick.

No! No! No! Stay back.

Maverick had to stop his dog from advancing closer in order to save him. *Think!*

A word came to mind. The special one Maverick had trained Wolf on to avoid danger. Austin had suggested it because he never wanted his dogs to be in harm's way.

"Wolf, retreat!" Maverick yelled as loud as he could, thankful that the attacker hadn't covered his mouth.

Wolf stopped and hopped onto the riverbank, changing directions. He barreled back toward the tree line in the same zigzag fashion and hid behind an enormous tree close to Maverick's location.

Seconds later, Violet appeared and positioned herself with Wolf. "Maverick!"

He had to keep her from getting any closer, but would his weakening, woozy brain allow for anything but a whisper? "Vi, stay back."

"Give it up, Santa Man," she yelled. "Police are on their way."

Good. Maverick needed their help. Was it true what they said? That your life flashed before your eyes when you were about to die? He didn't want to find out, but how could he survive what he guessed was about to happen?

Santa Man cussed. "Nope." He placed his hands under Maverick's body. "Time for you to swim. The ice won't hold you. Then I'm gonna kill your dog and girlfriend. Shame you won't be alive to see it."

"No!" Maverick's helpless word squeaked out.

"Goodbye." The criminal pushed.

Maverick cried out and tumbled down the steep incline. He lifted his feet and banged them into the ground, but it was no use. He couldn't stop his fall.

He registered Santa Man's laughter behind him as Maverick's body crashed onto the half-frozen lake.

Violet's piercing scream filtered through his tunnel-like fogginess as a shot rang out. *No! God, protect Violet and Wolf!*

Maverick willed her to save herself and his dog, but the words remained silent as his muscular weight broke through the ice.

And plunged him into the murky water.

ELEVEN

"No!" Violet scrambled toward the ice in the same zigzag fashion she'd seen Wolf run, praying the shooter would miss. She had to risk that the gunman would give up because Maverick's life depended on her getting him out of the water.

But how, with the lake's ice cracked in so many places? They'd have to approach from a different side of the hole. Hopefully, the ice was thicker there.

Wolf growled and hustled toward the shooter.

Another shot blasted throughout the wilderness before sirens sounded in the distance. Help was arriving, but would it be too late?

"I'll get you another time." The man sprinted to the tree line, retreating.

Good.

Wolf changed directions and headed to the location Violet had last seen Maverick before he fell. The dog stopped at the shoreline and barked, turning back to Violet.

As if beckoning her for help.

Her radio crackled. "Violet, come in."

Jill. She was alive.

Violet pushed the button. "Where are you? Need help. Mav in water." Her jumbled words made little sense. *Get it together. Maverick needs you to stay calm.*

"In the parking lot with the fire department, paramedics and Sara."

"Send them here now. Maverick fell through the ice at the

Talber Lake swimming hole. Shooter in the woods. Be careful and hurry!"

"On our way."

Thank You, Lord.

Wolf barked.

She couldn't wait. She had to do something. Violet hurried to the dock to the left of the steep incline Maverick had rolled down. Wolf followed her onto the wooden plank. She examined the area where Maverick fell through as her father's motto rang in her ears.

Keep your eyes to the skies and ears in nature.

Frank Hoyt had taught each of her siblings everything there was to know about the wilderness and mountainous area, including falling through ice. Maverick was a few meters from her position, but how could she reach him? A broken branch lay on the ice beside the dock, but she would have to venture onto the lake in order to get it. Would she be able to use it to help pull him out? She had to try.

The sound of water sloshing caught her attention.

Maverick's zip-tied hands broke through the lake's surface.

He was alive, but for how long? The freezing temperatures would send his body into shock soon. She was too far away for him to hear the instructions her father had taught her.

Violet cupped her hands around her mouth to boost the sound of what she had to tell him. "Maverick, get your hands on the ice and your feet out behind you."

He didn't respond.

Wolf crawled onto the ice, keeping himself low, and inched toward the hole.

Could Violet do the same without falling in? She had to test the thickness. She gingerly pressed her foot on the ice. It held. She placed her other one down, and repeated her test. *So far, so good.*

She slowly sank to her knees and crawled toward the branch. "Maverick! I'm coming."

His head appeared, and he spit out water. "Stay. Back. Too—" His teeth chattered, stopping his sentence.

She stayed a safe distance from the edge and noted his bound hands. Not good. Wait. A different idea formed. His knife was still in her pocket. She reached back and withdrew it.

Violet pressed the button and gently shimmied closer, holding her breath that she wouldn't fall in either. "Maverick, can you hoist your elbows onto the ice and hold out your hands? I need to cut your ties."

Shouts sounded behind her, but she kept her attention focused on Maverick. The others would never reach him in time.

He struggled, but finally found the strength to do as she asked and held out his hands.

She cut through the plastic. "Okay, listen closely. I'm going to give you the knife. Use it as an ice pick to haul yourself out of the hole. Kick your feet. When you're out, roll away from the hole. Got it?"

His fingers fumbled with the knife.

"Come on. You can do this, Mav." *Don't you dare leave me now. Not when you've reentered my life.*

"Violet, get back." Sara's voice bellowed from the shoreline.

Violet ignored her and wormed herself backward. She had to keep herself dry in order to help Maverick. "Try again, Mav!"

He jabbed the ice with his right hand, but slipped.

His limbs were weakening.

"You have to help me," she yelled. "Kick hard."

Maverick edged out of the icy prison.

"Wolf, pull," Violet commanded.

Wolf latched on to Maverick's collar with his teeth and towed his handler farther away from the hole.

"Now roll toward the shoreline, Mav! Wolf, come." Violet also rolled toward the dock.

Crack!

Violet stopped and held her breath. *Ice, don't fail me now.*

We're almost there. When no further cracks exploded, she continued.

Moments later, they reached the shore. Violet brought Maverick into an embrace, keeping him warm. "Sara, need paramedics."

Wolf nestled beside his handler, licking his face.

"Thank you for saving me." Maverick's whispered words could barely be heard over top of the shouts behind them. "Man—gun—shoot—Wolf…"

Violet placed her fingers over his lips. "Shhh. Don't talk. The shooter is gone. Raise your feet into the air. We need to get the water out of your boots."

Maverick complied.

Two firefighters appeared, crouching low. "I saw what you did," one said. "Someone taught you well, but you should have waited. It's dangerous."

She knew it was, but time wouldn't have allowed her the luxury. "I couldn't."

He nodded. "We've got him. Get to safety."

Violet released her grip on her freezing friend. "Be careful with him."

"We will, ma'am." The firefighters lifted Maverick to where the paramedics waited.

"Wolf, come," Violet commanded.

Together, they inched up the icy hill and stood beside Maverick.

Sara and Jill trotted in their direction.

Sara marched over to Violet and poked her in the chest. "Don't. Ever. Do. That. Again."

"I had to save him or he wouldn't have made it." Violet battled to find her breath.

"You should never have been out here in the first place. I told you to stay put." Sara didn't lower her panicked voice. "Why didn't you listen?"

"I know. I'm sorry, but we had to get here to find evidence

buried with the skeletal remains before they did. You saw the video." She reached into her pocket and brought out the necklace. "We found this. It's a flash drive."

Sara wiggled her fingers. "Give it to me. We'll get forensics to check it."

Violet dropped it into her friend's gloved hand. "Have you arrested Remi? Could she be Ragnovica? She was in the area when we were attacked two days ago."

"Let's not jump to conclusions yet. Everett is bringing her to the station. Vi, we don't have enough evidence to arrest her, but we'll get to the bottom of it. I promise." She hugged Violet. "I'm so glad you're okay."

Warmth spread into Violet's icy limbs. "Me, too. That was too close."

"What happened?" Jill asked.

Her question reminded Violet of her coworker's presence. Anger bubbled inside and Violet pushed on Jill's shoulders. "Where were you?" Suspicion prickled the back of her neck.

She thrust out her hand. "I cut myself and had to go to the park station for a first aid kit. I'm sorry."

Violet dug her toe boot into the snow. Her story didn't make sense, as she knew Jill always kept a kit in her vehicle, but why would she lie? Was she somehow involved?

No, Jill had never given Violet any reason to doubt her. She'd even stood up for her when Jesse ridiculed her in front of the other park workers.

"Vi!" Maverick's distraught cry ripped her out of thoughts of Jesse.

She rushed back to his side and spoke to the paramedics. "Is he okay?"

"He will be. We're taking him to the hospital, to be sure." He pointed to the board and spoke to his fellow paramedic. "Let's get him ready. We'll have to carry him out."

"Wait." Maverick clutched Violet's hand. "It was a trap to

take Wolf out. Get him back to the ranch. Ragnovica has now targeted him."

Once again, a chill sent ice darts throughout Violet's body. Everyone around her was in danger.

Even Wolf.

Maverick drew the plush plaid blanket snug under his chin and stretched his feet closer to the crackling warmth of the living room fireplace. The doctor at the hospital had done a thorough examination and discharged him midafternoon, saying Maverick was fortunate Violet had pulled him out of the water when she did. Any longer and it would have been a different story.

Wolf snuggled beside him on the couch. Sara had followed Violet and Wolf back to the ranch to ensure they arrived safely. Leaving Violet and Wolf in Buck's care, Sara had gone to the station to help Nick interrogate the reporter, Remi Meyer. Sara had returned to the ranch five minutes ago to give an update. She and Violet were in the kitchen making hot chocolate while Riley watched a Christmas movie in the den.

"Okay, here we go." Violet entered the room and handed him a snowman mug filled with hot chocolate, marshmallows, whipped cream and sprinkles. "I made Riley one, too."

"Are you trying to give her a sugar rush?" Maverick smirked and tasted the treat. "So good. What's in it?"

"Secret family recipe." She winked and sat in the rocking chair. "Sara, have you charged Remi?"

"Slow down, girl. Everett is checking her alibi." The constable positioned herself in the matching chair.

"Can you tell us what happened?" Maverick understood they weren't law enforcement, so sharing details of a case wasn't permitted.

"I checked with our sergeant and he was okay with giving you some information." She sipped her hot chocolate before continuing, "She denied everything and says what was caught on video was simply her talking to her cameraperson, Debb

Hughes. Apparently, a source gave her a tip that evidence was on the person buried in the forest."

"Who's her source?" Violet asked.

"She wouldn't divulge that information and before you ask, we don't know yet who the remains belong to. Dr. Patch and her team are currently extracting them now under police escort."

"Have they identified the person belonging to the head yet?" Violet placed her hot chocolate on a nearby end table and stoked the fire.

"Dr. Patch said Dr. Welborn is waiting to hear on dental records. They should know soon." She took another sip. "You really have to share this recipe."

"Not happening." Violet replaced the poker and sat back down. "What else can you tell us?"

"Only that Everett is checking out Remi's alibi with Debb and for the time of the Hancocks' disappearance two years ago. Remi claims she was at an all-day media event." Sara tapped her index finger on her chin. "But Vi, I'm leaning toward believing her. Plus, we don't know if Ragnovica is male or female. Sure, Remi can be ruthless in her reporting, but it's only so she'll get the scoop."

"I've heard that about her. Apparently, she's taken lots of risks for a story in the past." Violet cupped her hands around her mug and sipped.

"Oh, and Vi, digital forensics found spyware on your cell phone. That's how they got in."

"How did that happen?" Maverick asked.

"Carefully, but this spyware is expensive, and not just anyone could afford it."

"But a criminal mob boss probably could," Maverick said.

"Exactly. We're trying to find out where it was purchased, but it's a long shot. I'm guessing they found someone on the dark web selling it. It appears like they looked through her apps and contacts." Sara finished her hot chocolate and stood. "I need to go have a chat with Heather Kane before the end of my shift, but I wanted to give you an update and check to ensure you're okay." She leaned over and petted Wolf. "And to make sure this guy is well protected."

Violet's phone dinged. "That's an email. I gave it a chime sound. Let me check." She removed it from her pocket and swiped, jumping to her feet. "It's from Baylee."

"What does it say?" Maverick's curiosity piqued.

"Amy deserves justice. Don't trust her aunt." Violet's gaze shifted to Sara. "Seems Heather Kane has some explaining to do."

"And that's my cue to go there. See if you can find out where Baylee's hiding. Tell her we can protect her." She waggled a finger at Maverick. "You get better and make sure Violet stays put."

"I will, but you know how she can be, right?"

Sara nodded. "Stubborn."

Violet threw her hands in the air. "Hello, I'm in the room and can hear you."

Maverick chuckled. "Sara, you coming tonight? You can bring a date."

Violet moved closer to the couch. "Mav, are you sure you're feeling up to going to a party?"

"I'm fine and we need the distraction." He addressed Sara. "Well?"

"I'm coming, but no date. What's the dress code?"

"Casual to dressy, but not to the extreme." Maverick eyed Violet. "Do you need to get more clothes from your condo?"

"Right. I didn't bring anything fit to wear to a party. Sara, can you pick up a couple of dresses and throw in my cowboy boots?"

Sara cocked her head, raising a brow. "Which ones? You have like five pairs."

"Surprise me."

"Will do. Gotta run."

"Let me get my keys." She scurried out of the room.

Maverick threw off his blanket and slowly stood. Even though the doctor had discharged him, he wasn't feeling one hundred percent, but wasn't about to tell the girls that. "I'll walk you out."

Sara flattened her lips. "I'm serious about her being stubborn. Please don't let her leave. I'm counting on you."

"You two are close, aren't you?" He gestured her toward the foyer. "How did you meet?"

"Church, but lately she hasn't been attending. I'm worried."

"Why do you think she stopped?"

The doorbell rang.

"Not exactly sure, but I believe it has something to do with her mother and this was before she found out Erica had kept the fact that Violet had a twin a secret. She feels her mother is a hypocrite."

"That's harsh, even for Violet."

"Agree. Definitely out of character."

Hasty footfalls pounded on the foyer's hardwood floor, and Violet reappeared. She passed a set of keys to Sara. "Here you go."

"See you later."

"Call with updates. If you can." Maverick reached around her and opened the front door.

A woman in her late fifties stood on the veranda.

Behind him, Violet gasped. "Mom?"

Great. Would Erica Hoyt only add to their already heightened stress levels?

After saying goodbye to Sara, Violet escorted her mother into the dining room. Anger threatened to bubble to the surface. She closed the French doors connecting the dining room with the kitchen and turned to her mother. "Mom, why are you here?"

Erica Hoyt wiggled out of her coat and tossed it on a chair. "I had to see you. You haven't been answering my calls."

"I've been a tad busy." She steeled her jaw and softened her tone. "Mom, you didn't have to come. You're busy getting ready for the Hoyt family Christmas." And honestly, Violet desired a break from her smothering mother. She'd been hovering too much lately. Asking Violet why she wasn't attending church, if she'd been dating anyone, why she never came home to visit… The list went on.

"Not everyone can come this year. Would you consider coming home with me for Christmas?"

"Mom, I'm working. Right now, the mayor is counting on me to help find a young girl. I can't leave." Violet failed to quell the quiver in her voice.

Her mother took two long strides forward and hugged Violet. "I love how much you care and give everything to your job, but I'm worried about you. You've been distant lately."

Violet stiffened in her mother's embrace. "I'm fine, Mom. I have Maverick, Wolf and Sara to protect me."

Her mother retreated, her eyes clouding. "I guess you don't need me. I'll get going."

And…there it was. The infamous mother guilt trip. "Mom, it's not that I don't want you here. I'm just having a hard time understanding why you kept Baylee a secret."

She placed her hands on Violet's shoulders. "I told you. I was protecting you from the loss." She chewed on her bottom lip. "Twins run in our family and I lost my twin when I was five. Erin and I were in the car when my mother had an accident. I survived. Erin didn't." Erica Hoyt's pain was evident in her whispered words. "I understand what it's like to have a twin ripped away. Part of me died that day."

Violet's heart softened, and she hugged her mom. "I'm sorry. Why didn't you tell us?"

"I'm not sure. I still find it hard to think about that time in my life." She held Violet at arm's length. "I realize you never met your twin, Baylee. But I didn't want you to go through even a morsel of that pain. Can you forgive me?"

"I'm getting there and I'm sorry you lost your twin, but now you understand why I must find Baylee. Mom, she's been emailing me."

Erica Hoyt's eyes grew wide. "She's in the area?" She gripped Violet's hand. "Then you must find her. I need to meet my other beautiful daughter."

"I'm working on it. She's been giving me clues about what's going on with these criminals."

"What? She's putting herself in danger. Do you have any idea where she could be?"

Violet shook her head and explained the situation, including the need to find the missing Hancock girl. "Mom, so you see why I can't leave right now? Maverick will keep me safe."

Her mother smiled. "I'm so glad he's back in your life. I always liked him. Such a polite man."

And here we go. "Mom, don't start."

"What?"

"I hear the matchmaking tone in your voice." Violet crossed her arms. "Maverick and I are only friends."

Riley's laughter filtered into the dining room.

Her mother fixated her attention on the French doors. "Who's that?"

"Riley. Maverick's daughter."

Her mother's eyes widened again. "He has a daughter?"

"Yup, and he only just found out about her. Pray for him. Riley is having a hard time warming up to him and it's been tough." Violet smiled as Riley burst out with another fit of laughter. "She's so cute, Mom."

"Can't wait to meet her." Her mother checked her watch. "I best go find a hotel and head back tomorrow morning. I had to see you in person to make sure you're okay."

"Mom, there's plenty of room here."

"I don't want to impose."

"I'm sure Buck and Maverick won't mind. Plus, they're having a party tonight. It will be fun. I'll—"

Her cell phone played Christmas bells. Violet fished it from her pocket and checked the screen. Dr. Welborn. "I have to take this. Just a sec." She hit Answer. "Violet Hoyt speaking."

"Violet, I have news. The mayor demanded I keep you updated. I've already called Constable Daley." A pause.

Violet held her breath. "What is it?"

"Dental records came back on the skull. It's Tanya Ryan. Apparently, she was Amy's nanny. Appears that the remains were in the forest for just over a year."

"So, not as long as the others?"

"Correct."

Odd. Why the time difference?

Violet rubbed her neck muscles. "Do you know how she died?"

"Gunshot wound to the head. I've reached out to the person on her emergency contact list. Heather Kane."

Violet drew in a sharp breath. That couldn't be a coincidence. Was Heather somehow involved?

TWELVE

After getting Violet's mother settled into the other guest room, Maverick reclined as Riley put together a puzzle. Wolf had nestled beside her, casually watching her every move with one eye open. The two had bonded quickly. Too bad Maverick couldn't say the same thing about his daughter's response to himself. Even though Riley had warmed up to everyone else at the ranch, she was still standoffish with him. *Piper, why did you keep her a secret from me?* Regret washed over him at the lost years. Five years that he could have spent nurturing their relationship and earning her trust. Heat flushed his face. *Mav, move on. Your anger isn't helping Riley now.*

"Ugh!" The five-year-old chucked a handful of pieces across the room.

Wolf stirred from his slumber-like state.

"What's wrong, Pumpkin?" Maverick threw off his blanket.

She pouted. "I can't do it."

Maverick pushed himself up. "How about we build the puzzle together?" He gathered the pieces and sat on the floor, cross-legged, at the coffee table. He lifted a piece. "Let me see." He hovered the item over the picture she'd half finished as he made a choo choo train sound, inserting it in the appropriate spot. "There."

Her eyes brightened, and she giggled before picking up another piece, handing it to him. "Again."

He completed the puzzle by repeating the process, while Riley interjected at different moments. When they finished, she clapped and squealed. "Yay!"

"See, that wasn't too hard. It's better when we do it together." Would this be a good time to talk to his daughter? *Lord, give me the words.* "Pumpkin, I want you to know that Daddy only found out about you when you came to live here." He clutched her hand. "I would have visited you long before now. I love you."

Riley's eyelids fluttered. "Me, too, Daddy." She pointed to the next puzzle. "Another?"

Had Maverick turned a corner with his daughter? Who would have thought it would start with something as simple as puzzle-building?

Two complete puzzles later, Erica and Violet entered the room.

Riley skipped to Violet and hugged her legs. "See what I did with Daddy?"

Daddy. Not Mister. His daughter was beginning to trust him. Finally.

Violet's gaze snapped to Maverick's, her mouth dropping before speaking to Riley. "That's awesome. They're so pretty."

Riley pointed to Erica. "Who's this?"

Maverick uncrossed his cramped legs. He placed his hands on the armrest and pushed himself to his feet, using the couch as leverage. "Honey, this is Vi's mommy, Mrs. Hoyt."

Erica bent over and stuck out her hand. "You can call me Mrs. Erica. Nice to meet you, Riley."

Maverick's daughter shook the older woman's hand. "Hi."

The doorbell rang.

"That's Sara and Nick," Violet said. "They have information for us."

Maverick tipped his chin toward his daughter. "Mrs. Hoyt, would you be able to get Riley a cookie from the snowman jar in the kitchen?"

"Of course." Erica extended her hand to Riley. "How about a treat, young lady?"

The redhead turned up her nose. "I'm a girl. Not a lady."

The group chuckled as Erica escorted Riley into the kitchen.

"Wow. Seems you're getting along with her," Violet whispered as they walked to the front door.

"Yes, we may have bonded over a puzzle." He harrumphed. "I wish I'd known that earlier, but I'll take it. Let's hope it continues."

"I have a good feeling."

Maverick opened the door. A gust of wind blew in a cloud of powdery snow, chilling Maverick's bones. "Come in, guys."

The duo entered, and Sara handed Violet a bag. "Here are your party clothes and boots."

Maverick motioned down the hall. "Let's go into the living room by the fire."

Nick removed his hat. "Sounds good to me. I just spent thirty minutes shoveling an older woman's walkway."

"Is that one of your duties?" Violet asked.

"Sometimes." Nick approached the fireplace, took off his gloves and held his hands close to the burning logs. "Aww, so much better."

Maverick's phone dinged, and he read the text. "Oh good. Austin and Izzy will be here in time for tonight's party."

Violet plunked into the rocking chair. "Sorry to rush you, but us girls need to get ready. Tell us what you found out."

"Yes, and I have to get home to change." Sara withdrew her notebook. "We'll keep it short. We could have called to tell you this, but since I had to drop off your clothes, we thought we'd do it in person on our way back into town. As I suspected, Remi's alibi was confirmed on both accounts. From a couple days ago as well as the Hancock murders two years ago."

Maverick shook his head. "So, all she's guilty of is looking for a story?"

"You got it."

"What about Heather Kane?" Violet asked.

"I can answer that." Nick retreated from the fireplace. "She claims someone stole her van and that Tanya Ryan is her late husband's estranged half sister. Apparently, Heather got Tanya the job, but then they had a falling-out over family matters."

"Do you think she's telling the truth?" Violet bit her lower lip.

The nervous habit he remembered from university, but one Maverick thought made her even prettier.

"At first, but when we showed her the necklace and asked if she could identify it, she clammed up. She said she'd never seen it before."

"You said they were estranged. Maybe she truly doesn't know." Violet fiddled with the tassels on her hoodie.

Nick shrugged. "My cop gut is telling me otherwise. I'm going to monitor her. I'm not buying her innocence yet."

Violet leaned forward, clasping her hands. "Any word on the Calgary location of Asterbine Shipping?"

"Constable Porter got the same response I did here when I went to their office," Sara said. "We had to talk to their lawyers. They wouldn't give any information on their business without a warrant."

Violet scowled. "Figures."

"Vi, have you heard any more from Baylee?" Sara asked.

Violet snatched her laptop from an end table. "I emailed her earlier to see if she would tell me where she is. Let me check." She ran her finger over the touchpad, bringing her computer to life, and read her sister's message. "She won't say. Says it's for my protection."

"Not surprised." Sara checked her watch. "Time to hit the road."

Violet's hand flew to her mouth. "She just sent another cryptic email."

Sara stood. "What does it say?"

Violet turned her screen so they could read it.

Going silent for both of our sakes. Trust no one. Ragnovica could be anyone and has threatened to kill us both.

Maverick sucked in a breath. How much longer before this Ragnovica found Violet? He had to stay close, as he wouldn't lose her again.

Not after just finding her.

Violet shivered. Not just from the cold day, but from her sister's latest warning. She rubbed her arms to spread warmth throughout her body, but it was useless. Good thing the barn was heated. Thankfully, her mother was the same size as Violet, so she would wear one of the dresses Sara had brought.

Violet observed herself in the full-length mirror. The red-and-green plaid dress was perfect for the occasion. Her green cowboy boots completed her ensemble nicely. Time to help Riley get ready.

After all, this was her first Christmas party with her daddy, and Violet wanted the little girl to dazzle Maverick.

Violet left her room and knocked on Riley's door. "Honey, can I come in?"

"Yes." The faint, one-word reply betrayed the little girl's sorrowful mood.

Violet eased the door open.

Riley sat on her bed, tears rolling down her cheeks.

Violet brought her into an embrace. "Honey, what's wrong?"

Her bright blue eyes glistened with tears in the dimmed lighting. "Miss—Mama." She sniffed in between words.

"I know, sweetie. It's so hard, but remember what your daddy said."

She blinked tears away. "What?"

Violet tapped her finger on Riley's chest. "Mommy will always be in your heart."

She bit her lip. "Would you be my new mama?"

Violet's insides melted like a marshmallow roasting over red-hot coals. This little girl had stolen Violet's heart. There was no turning back now. She had to stay connected with Maverick if she was going to see Riley. "Oh sweetie, no one could ever replace your mama." Violet pushed a disheveled curl from Riley's face. "But I will be your friend. Would you like that?"

She nodded.

"Good." Violet noted the dresses lying on the floor. "How about we get you ready for Daddy's party?"

She sprang off the bed. "Yes! Can you do my hair like yours?"

"Of course." Violet stood and scooped up the dresses. "Now, which one of these shall we choose?"

Riley pointed.

"Aww...perfect. We'll match."

Twenty minutes later, Violet held Riley's hand and followed Erica Hoyt into the toasty, warm barn.

Buck greeted them, tipping his cowboy hat. "Howdy, gals. Don't you all look purty tonight? Welcome to my ranch Christmas ball." He chuckled. "Well, that's what I call it. Not fit for kings and queens, but all are welcome."

Violet scanned the large, open room. Lights adorned the rafters and beams. Tinsel, intertwined with pine branches, was strung around each column. Tables of food lined one wall while a Christmas tree with multicolored lights glowed in the corner. Christmas songs played in the background.

A perfect setting to take their minds off the criminal mastermind stalking them. But for how long?

She returned her focus to the man in charge. "It's beautiful, Buck. What did you do with the horses?"

The stalls to the right were empty.

"Moved them to the rear of the barn." He waved his hand toward the table. "Help yourself. There's plenty to eat."

"Don't mind if I do." Violet's mother meandered over to the food and joined Sara, who was pouring herself some eggnog.

Maverick approached.

And Violet couldn't help the soft intake expelling out of her mouth. He was dressed in jeans, a brown plaid shirt, cowboy hat and boots. The perfect cowboy.

The father had stolen Violet's heart as much as his daughter had. *Vi, rein it in. You're not here for romance.*

He stopped a few yards away and whistled. "Wow. Look at the two most beautiful women at the ball. You match."

Violet smiled. The response she had hoped he'd give when he saw his fun-loving daughter. Violet had piled Riley's red curls on the top of her head and added gold bows. The five-year-old had picked the red plaid dress and black satin shoes.

"Miss Vi and I look alike." Riley's cheerful tone matched her smile. Her former tears had vanished.

Good. Maverick could use a win with this little girl.

He squatted in front of his daughter and hugged her. "Yes, you do. You're beautiful, Pumpkin."

She wiggled out of his arms. "What about Miss Vi? Does she get a hug, too?"

Maverick stood. "Of course she does." He nabbed Violet's hand and twirled her before bringing her into his arms. "You look beautiful," he whispered in her ear.

Violet hitched in a breath—not only from his comment, but from the woodsy scent that surrounded her in his tight hold. *I could get used to his arms around me.*

Wait—where had that thought come from? *Focus. He only wants to be friends. Nothing more. And remember Jesse.*

She swallowed her crush and retreated from his embrace. "And you, fine sir, clean up nicely."

He dipped the brim of his cowboy hat, bowing slightly. "Why, thank you, ma'am."

The double doors opened, and a couple entered, followed by an Alaskan malamute.

Wolf barked and trotted to greet them.

"Austin!" Maverick turned to Violet. "Come meet my brother." He tugged Riley toward the pair before yanking his brother into a bear hug. "So good to see you." He hugged the beautiful woman. "Izzy, you, too."

The malamute barked.

Maverick ruffled the dog's fur. "You as well, Névé."

The two dogs woofed and wrestled as if that was their way of greeting friends.

Maverick nudged Riley forward. "Guys, I'd like you to meet my daughter, Riley." He turned to the five-year-old. "Riley, this is your Uncle Austin and Aunt Izzy, and their dog, Névé. Her name means snow in another language."

Riley curtsied, surprising Violet.

And from the look on Maverick's face—him, too.

"Nice to meet you," Riley said.

"You, too, young lady. We're happy you're in our family." Austin stuck his hand out.

She shook it. "Can I pet your dog?"

Izzy took off her coat and bent low. "You sure can, but can I have a hug first?" She held open her arms.

Riley walked into her, snuggling close before she jerked back. "Your belly feels funny."

Izzy glanced at Austin. "Is it finally time to share?"

He nodded and turned to Maverick. "We waited a bit before sharing this news. You're gonna be an uncle."

Maverick clasped his brother's shoulder. "Congratulations."

"Thanks, bro." Austin retreated and eyed Violet, sticking out his hand. "Sorry, I'm being rude. You must be Violet."

She returned the handshake. "I am. Nice to meet you and Izzy. Congratulations on your news. That's exciting."

"Mav told us what's going on," Izzy whispered. "I'm a police officer and can offer my help if you need it."

"Thank you." She beckoned Sara to come and join them.

Sara approached.

"This is Constable Sara Daley," Violet said. "She's also my best friend."

The women shook hands.

Izzy leaned close, out of earshot of the others. "Perhaps we can chat later. I know I'm not in your jurisdiction, but an extra set of eyes and ears always helps."

"Totally agree," Sara said. "I'd—"

The sound of stomping hooves and horse whinnies filtered through the barn, drowning out the music.

Wolf barked, then growled.

Névé did the same.

An odor assaulted Violet's nose. The source of the dogs' agitation.

Smoke.

Violet's heart rate increased, and her gaze shifted to the entrance.

Flames shot under the wooden doors.

The barn was on fire.

NO!

Had Ragnovica found her?

Now they were all in danger.

THIRTEEN

"Everyone, out!" Maverick lifted a whimpering Riley. "It's gonna be okay, Pumpkin. Daddy's got you. Austin, get the doors."

His brother scampered to the entrance and pushed, but the door didn't budge. "They're blocked. Is there another way out?"

Buck appeared at their side, out of breath. "The back doors are also jammed shut."

Flames had crawled up the barn's sides and now flickered in both windows. The fire would soon engulf them.

And everyone inside would perish.

Izzy called 911, asking for emergency services at their location.

Maverick passed Riley to Violet. "Keep her close. I need to help Austin." He rubbed his daughter's back. "It's going to be okay."

She extended her hand, reaching for him. "No, Daddy. Don't go like Mama."

Tears prickled the back of Maverick's eyes. He hated to leave his daughter, but had to find a way out to save her. Just like on a plane, he had to put his own mask on first, then help his loved ones. "It will be okay, Pumpkin. I'm not going anywhere." He cupped her little face in his hands. "Stay with Miss Vi, okay? I'll be back." He turned to Violet. "Stay low to the ground and find something to cover both of your mouths."

He couldn't lose Violet either. Now that she was back in his life, he wouldn't let her go.

She nodded, lowering her and Riley to the ground. Her

mother dipped the cloth napkins she held into a glass of water on the table and handed them to her. "Here. Use these."

Wolf barked.

Maverick turned to see what his dog was alerting to.

The Malinois scampered up the steps to the hayloft.

Buck latched on to Maverick's arm. "Smart dog. We can go to the loft and down the hay shaft. Open the doors from the outside. Quick, before the smoke rises more."

"Austin, you stay here. Once we get the doors open, help everyone out." Maverick wasn't about to lose the ranch he had worked so hard to get. Or, more importantly, the family God had given him.

He bounded up the steps with Buck at his heels. "Stay low."

The coughing below them intensified, along with Maverick's heartbeat. They were running out of time.

Wolf clawed at the hayloft doors, barking.

"Let's get the doors opened, Buck." Maverick lifted the steel bar holding the small entrance shut.

The pair each grabbed a panel and thrust it open.

Wolf immediately jumped through the opening and climbed onto the hay shaft, inching his way down.

Maverick crawled out and followed the same path as his dog, but not as quickly. *Lord, help us get the doors open in time.*

Moments later, Maverick and Buck reached the front. Flames crawled up both sides of the barn. If they didn't act fast, the structure would be gone.

Think, Mav. An idea formed.

Maverick ignored the icy chill snaking up his spine and scooped an armful of snow. He threw it on the doors.

The flames sizzled. Buck joined him, and soon they had stopped the fire on the door.

They yanked out the shovel someone had wedged through the handles to bar the door shut.

Maverick gently eased his hand on the handle, testing it. He jerked his fingers back and gathered more snow, rubbing it on the surface. It would have to do. He couldn't wait any longer.

"Buck, go to the back entrance so we can get the horses out that way."

The older man nodded and raced around the corner.

Maverick thrust open the doors and smoke assaulted him. He ducked and entered, crouch-walking. "Everyone, out!" Maverick fought his way through the thick cloud of smoke. "Violet! Riley! Where are you?"

He searched through the haze, but failed to spot the pair. Others sped past him, fleeing the fire. Ranch hands ushered the horses out the back entrance.

Blood whooshed in his ears, spreading panic through his exhausted body. *Keep it together. You have lives to save.*

"Maverick, over here!" Violet's voice filtered through the smoggy barn.

He followed the sound and reached her within seconds. Sara, Riley, Erica and Violet were huddled together. He took Riley from Violet. "Everyone, stay low and follow me."

Wolf barked. He had joined his handler back into the fire.

"Wolf, protect and retreat," Maverick commanded.

The dog tugged on the bottom of Violet's dress.

"Good boy. Violet, grab Wolf by the collar. Let him lead you out."

"Mom, take my other hand. We'll go out together." Violet hooked her fingers into the dog's collar and clutched her mother's hand. "Sara, let's go."

Sara stayed close to the group. Safety in numbers.

"Wolf, go." Maverick followed his dog as he led them through the fire.

They reached outside, and the group dropped into the snow, struggling for breaths.

Sirens pierced the night.

Riley cried in his arms. He held her tighter. "It's okay, Pumpkin. We're out."

"Horseys?"

"Uncle Buck is getting them out." Maverick eyed the ranch hands at the front of the barn. One held a water hose on the flames while others threw piles of snow on top. They were trying to slow the flames before the fire trucks arrived.

Austin approached with Izzy and Névé. "You guys okay?"

Maverick nodded. "You?"

"Yes," Izzy said. "I asked for ambulances. The paramedics will check on everyone for smoke inhalation."

"How did this happen?" Sara asked. "I thought the Hawkweed River Ranch's perimeter was secure."

"It was." Maverick shifted his attention to the driveway. "We locked down the gate once all guests arrived."

"Well, then, we'll need to question everyone." Sara turned to Izzy. "You up for a little interrogation?"

"Sure am. Mav, we need to keep everyone here."

"You think those responsible live at the ranch?" Maverick knew for a fact Buck vetted every employee. "Most of the staff are ex-military and Buck trusts them."

"Someone not only started the fire, but barricaded us inside." Sara gestured toward the crowd. "Money talks and can be a tremendous temptation to some."

"Not my ranch hands." Buck had approached quietly. "I trust them with my life."

"How could anyone gain access?" Erica asked.

Violet's eyes widened. "A hacker could."

"She's right," Maverick said. "They could have hacked into the security system and disarmed the gate to let someone breach the property."

Buck pulled out his cell phone and tapped on it, his eyes narrowing. "It's disarmed, and I didn't do it. Why didn't I get an alert?"

"I'm guessing the hacker disabled the notification system, too." Maverick gritted his teeth.

"Who all has access, Buck?" Izzy asked.

"Me, Maverick and my lead ranch hand."

Sara spoke to Buck. "I need one of your rifles. I'm going to scour the perimeter until emergency personnel arrive."

"I can help. Do you have more than one?" Izzy asked.

"Sure do. Come with me." Buck beckoned them to follow. "Mav, you guide the fire trucks in."

Sirens grew louder and Riley squirmed in his arms. "Don't be scared, Pumpkin. They're here to help."

Flashing lights illuminated the area.

Riley nestled closer. "No. Mama. No. Help."

What was his daughter referring to?

Violet rubbed Riley's back. "Let me take her. You go talk to the firefighters."

"Thank you." Once again, Maverick placed Riley into Violet's trustworthy custody.

Riley wrapped her arms around Violet's neck like a life jacket.

Something about the sirens and flashing lights scared his daughter, raising a question.

Had she been in the car when Piper was killed?

He pushed the thought and his shaky emotions aside before trudging through the snow toward the approaching vehicles—until a flash of movement brought him to a halt.

Wolf and Névé barked in unison.

A shadow skulked through the trees.

Someone had indeed breached the Hawkweed River Ranch.

And now Maverick's family was in mortal danger.

Violet stiffened at the dogs' heightened barks and growls. Something—or someone—caught both dogs' attention.

Maverick pivoted and pointed to the tree line. "Wolf, get 'em!"

The dog scurried through the snow at an incredible speed.

A shot rang out as a cruiser sped into the laneway.

"Take cover," Maverick yelled.

"Mom, head to the trees." Violet placed her hand on the back of Riley's head, holding her close, and dashed toward the closest cluster of pines. Violet refused to let the horror of the situation engulf her. She must protect the little girl in her arms. Riley was priority—not Violet.

Others scurried around the property. *God, keep us safe.*

Violet huddled with her mother. "Why does this keep happening? Where is God in all of this, Mom?"

"Beside us. Around us. Behind us. He's everywhere, Vi. You just have to trust."

Riley whimpered in Violet's hold, drawing her attention to the fragile little one who'd recently lost her mother. The conversation about God would have to wait. Violet couldn't risk subjecting Riley to more conflict than she had already endured. "Shhh, Daddy will protect us."

But who would keep Maverick safe?

Wolf's bark reminded Violet of the amazing weapon at Maverick's disposal.

A flash of white fur caught her eye. Névé had joined in pursuing the intruder.

Shouts mingled with the sirens blared throughout the property. There was no way the suspect would escape all this. Unless—

Someone on the Hawkweed River Ranch had betrayed them all.

Had Ragnovica sent men to take them out, including Wolf? The criminal mastermind had tried before.

Another shot rang out, followed by Sara's loud command, "Police, stand down!"

Wolf and Névé growled.

Violet peeked around the tree trunk.

Sara and Izzy stood over a man lying in the snow, their weapons trained on him.

Wolf and Névé surrounded the group, baring their teeth in a unified front, protecting the property.

Moments later, Violet scanned the area. Firefighters doused

the flames as ranch hands herded the horses into the nearby paddock. So much for a fun evening of celebrating Christmas.

But thankfully, Maverick and Buck had acted quickly, or the barn would have been destroyed.

At least there was that.

Maverick approached them. "Get to the house. Austin and I will round up the dogs. Can you take Riley and watch her, Vi?"

"Of course. Where are you going?"

"I want to see how the suspect got onto the property, but I need Riley inside, where it's safe." He kissed his daughter's soot-infested forehead. "I'll be in to tuck you in bed, Pumpkin."

Violet loved Maverick's tenderness toward his daughter. The man's gentle ways were melting the icy shield Violet had constructed around her heart after Jesse's destructive carnage.

"Perhaps Miss Vi will help you with your letter to Santa." Maverick tweaked her nose. "Would you like that?"

Leave it to him to turn an ugly situation into something fun. She had always loved that playful side of him.

Riley pouted. "But I can't write."

Violet tucked a fallen red curl behind the little girl's ear. "I will help you. And if it's okay with Daddy, maybe we can have a gingerbread cookie and milk."

"Is it, Daddy?"

"Of course. I'll be in soon." Maverick turned to his K-9. "Wolf, protect."

The dog settled beside Violet and Riley like a sentinel in the night, committing to watch over his wards.

The redhead rested her head on Violet's shoulders, obviously trusting both the woman who held her and the dog sent to guard her.

Violet walked by Izzy and Sara as they questioned the assailant. It wasn't Santa Man. Another Ragnovica henchman? They seemed to slither out of the woodwork.

The man sneered at Violet, his eyes flashing fire darts her

way. "You can't hide forever. She will get to you again, and then your nine lives will expire."

She?

Wolf growled, baring his teeth.

The man staggered backward. "Don't trust anyone." His gaze shifted to Sara. "Not even those close to you."

What did that mean? Was Ragnovica a woman?

Sara tightened her grip, thrusting his arm upward at an awkward angle.

He cried out and mumbled curse words.

"Next time, I won't be as pleasant. You're going away, mister." She shoved him toward the idling cruiser and turned back. "I'll call you later, Vi."

"Thanks." Violet gritted her teeth at the hostile exchange and trudged up the ranch's steps. "Time for cookies, Riley?"

She lifted her head. "No more bad man?"

"That's right. Miss Sara is locking him up. You're safe now." *At least, I hope so.*

Riley laid her head back on Violet's shoulder.

Thirty minutes later, after having her cookie and milk, Riley sat at the kitchen table coloring on the Dear Santa letter Violet had written for her. Violet chuckled as the five-year-old recited her wants and wishes. *Oh, to be a child again at Christmas.*

Violet studied the redhead from her position at the kitchen's island, her own heart breaking at the thought of leaving the little girl. After all, once Ragnovica was captured and put behind bars, Violet would return to her humdrum life at her condo. At least she had Marmalade.

Though grateful for what she'd received, Violet secretly longed for a loving husband and a large family.

"You've fallen for her, haven't you?" Violet's mother placed a hot cup of tea in front of Violet and sat.

"Am I that obvious?" Violet lifted the string attached to the tea bag and dunked it multiple times. "She's hard to resist."

"And her father?" Erica Hoyt's eyes glistened as she smirked before sipping her tea.

Marmalade trotted into the room and hopped onto Violet's lap. "Mom, it's not like that." She petted her cat as it purred.

"The way you look at him when he's not looking tells me otherwise."

Violet snatched a cookie and leaned closer. "Shhh. Riley will hear you." She paused. "Mom, you know what Jesse did to me. I can't risk opening my heart to another man."

The woman huffed and sat back. "I never liked Jesse. I sensed something was off when you first introduced him to us. Your father thought that, too."

"And you said nothing? Mom, you could have stopped me from a boatload of hurt." Not to mention the scar on her abdomen.

Her mother raised a brow. "You seriously think you would have listened? Love blinded you from seeing what everyone else did."

Violet set her mug down. *Here we go, the guilt trip and chastising.* "Mom, I don't need a lecture right now."

She reached across the island and squeezed Violet's hand. "You're right, and I'm sorry. I didn't come here to fight, but to ask your forgiveness for not telling you about your twin."

"Baylee, Mom. Her name is Baylee." Violet failed to squash the anger in her voice.

"Miss Vi?"

Ugh. Now you've gone and done it. "See what you made me do?" She nudged Marmalade off her lap and walked over to Riley. "Did you finish?"

"I'll take my tea into the living room." Her mother leaned close. "I would like to see the old Violet. The happy one. Not this one." She sailed out of the room.

Violet resisted the urge to run after her mother, regretting her tantrum. As much as she hated to admit it, Violet's mother was right. *You have to shake this foul mood.*

Normally, the woman her friends knew was fun-loving and cheerful, but lately Violet had changed.

I want that Violet back, too, Mom.

"Do you like my picture to Santa, Miss Vi?"

Riley's question drew Violet's attention to the little girl who had stolen her heart. "Let me see." Violet inspected the child's drawing.

Riley had attempted to draw two tall figures, each holding on to a little girl's hands. A dog and cat sat beside them.

"It's beautiful. Who are these people?"

"You, me, Daddy, Marmy and Wolf, silly."

Violet's breath hitched. One happy family.

The family Violet wanted.

But could never have.

Violet hauled her blanket closer and cuddled by the fireplace, studying the Christmas tree in the corner. Maverick had returned and taken Riley to bed, promising to read her a Christmas story. Violet loved that daughter and father were growing closer. If only she and her mother could do the same.

Violet's mother had retreated to her room after Maverick had given them the all clear. Firefighters had extinguished the remaining embers and checked all the buildings. Paramedics had treated everyone. In case someone had hacked into their system, like they suspected, Buck had changed the passwords and codes to ensure it wouldn't happen again. The ranch was safe once more and under protection, with cruisers periodically patrolling the area.

Izzy, Austin and Névé had turned in for the night. They were staying in the bigger cabin on the east side of the property.

Wolf lay nestled beside her on the couch, protecting her from any more predators. She rubbed his fur. "You're a good dog."

"Of course he is." Maverick entered the room and sat across from the duo. "Thank you for looking after Riley."

"My pleasure. She's adorable."

"She is. Tonight terrified her, though."

"A fire can do that, especially if you're a five-year-old." Violet stared at the burning logs.

"Something else scared her tonight."

Violet sat straighter. "More than the fire and a scary-looking suspect? What do you mean?"

"The sirens and flashing lights made her more agitated." Maverick set his phone on the end table.

"What are you thinking?"

"That I would like to investigate Piper's accident closer. I'm wondering if Riley was in the car. The police didn't give me many details."

Violet drew in a sharp breath. "Oh, my. I'm sure Sara can help."

"I was thinking of talking to Izzy about it instead. Sara is really busy with the case."

"Good point." Violet threw off the blanket and stood, moving to the window. She parted the blinds and peered out.

Coin-sized snowflakes fluttered to the ground like a shaken snow globe. "It's snowing and is so pretty." She turned back to him. "Are you sure it's safe on the grounds?"

"Yes."

"Do they know how the fire started?"

"The fire chief found a discarded gas can on the other side of the barn. He informed the police, and Sara promised to give an update soon."

Violet returned to her spot on the couch. "Do you feel this was another one of Ragnovica's henchmen? Makes me wonder how many are out there."

"Not sure I want to know." Maverick yawned. "Where's your mother?"

"In her room. I'm afraid we had a bit of a fight earlier." Violet chewed on her lower lip.

"That's not good and you're doing it again."

"Doing what?"

"Chewing on your lower lip. Something you did all the time at university when you were anxious."

Violet sighed. "I can't seem to break that bad habit."

"I'm guessing this has to do with Baylee." Maverick got up and sat beside her. "Vi, don't do what I did when I found out my mother had kept Austin a secret."

"What do you mean?"

"I let my bitterness fester until a wise man at her church told me to put the past where it belonged. In the past." Maverick picked up the blanket and tucked it around Violet, gazing into her eyes. "It's not worth it. Your mother is still alive and loves you." He caressed her face.

Once again, Violet's breath hitched at his gentleness.

He leaned closer. "Vi, I need—"

Her cell phone dinged a text message, breaking the moment. She fished out the device. "That must be Sara." She swiped to bring her screen to life. "Nope, it's Dr. Patch. Thought she didn't text."

Got a tip Amy's body was buried north of where you found the babysitter's skull. Meet me there tomorrow and don't mess this up.

Violet drew in a ragged breath and turned the screen so Maverick could read it.

"Wait, what tip?"

Suspicion of the woman's mysterious tip knotted Violet's muscles, sending the attacker's earlier warning flashing into her mind.

Don't trust anyone. Not even those close to you.

Plus, he had said *she*.

Who was the man referring to?

FOURTEEN

Maverick drove into Asterbine National Park's station early the next morning and parked beside Sara's cruiser. "Good, she's here to protect us. I don't like that we're heading into the cold wilderness. My gut is telling me it's a trap, especially after you mentioned the suspect indicated that Ragnovica was a female. Do you think Dr. Patch could be involved?"

Violet put on her tuque. "She can be harsh, but a criminal? Doubtful."

Maverick cut the engine. "More bad weather is moving in, so we best get this done. I want to be home in time to help Riley put together another puzzle."

"I'm so glad she's warming up to you. I'm sure it's been tough becoming an instant father."

"I still can't shake the feeling that she was in the car when the accident happened. Oddly enough, none of the online articles mentioned that anyone else was in the car. Izzy suggested counseling as Riley may have suppressed the memory."

A vehicle approached.

"That's possible." Violet checked the parking lot. "Jill's here. Good. Let's go."

Maverick climbed out of his SUV and opened the rear, letting Wolf out of his cage. "Wolf, down."

The dog complied but stayed beside his handler. "Good boy." Maverick attached his leash. "Come."

The duo followed Violet and Jill into the park station.

The foyer was bustling with law enforcement, park wardens

and other members of the community. Even Mayor Coble stood in the corner speaking with a tall, bearded man.

Violet stopped. "Jill, why is Supervisor McGregor here?"

"No idea. Checking up on us?"

"I'm guessing your boss is the one talking to the mayor?" Maverick asked.

"Yup." Violet waved her hand toward a fortysomething woman approaching them. "That's Heather Kane. Watch what you say. I don't trust her after what Sara told us."

"Ms. Hoyt, I wanted to talk to you." Heather latched on to Violet's arm. "Please, find Amy. I need to put my entire family to rest."

Wolf growled.

Heather jerked back, raising her hands. "Whoa. I saw Remi's footage of this dog."

"So you know what he's capable of?" Maverick held on to his K-9 tightly.

Violet leaned closer. "Ms. Kane, are you somehow involved in Amy's disappearance?"

"No! I would never have hurt Amy or my sister's family."

Before Violet could respond, a park warden clapped, then whistled. "Okay, everyone, listen up." He waited for the murmurs to subside before continuing, "Since the mayor put out a call for help to find Amy Hancock, we're going to take advantage of it, but we're limited in time. This incoming storm is gonna pack a punch, so we've divided you into groups to search the northern part of the park. Because of a tip, that's where we're concentrating our efforts. Let's finally find Amy so the family can rest." He turned to the mayor. "Sir, do you want to say anything?"

Mayor Coble waited for the crowd to settle. "Thank you, Warden Irving. Listen, I'm sorry for calling you out here this close to Christmas, but this is personal for me. My daughter hasn't come out of the house since Amy went missing two years ago." He scanned the room. "I know this sounds selfish, but many of you are parents. You understand what it's like. Will you help us find Amy? Give her aunt and my daughter the gift of closure for Christmas?"

He gestured toward a table along one wall. "I've donated food, water, hats and mittens for your search out there in this weather."

The crowd stirred, and Maverick cast an eye over the group. Could Ragnovica be among those gathered, in disguise?

"Mayor Coble, are we any closer to finding out who killed the Hancock family?" Remi motioned for her cameraperson to follow.

Sara marched toward the duo. "Now isn't the time, Remi."

The crowd mumbled.

Mayor Coble held up his hands. "Let me answer. I want to assure the public that our constables are doing everything to apprehend those responsible. I want to send you all out with a prayer. Please bow your heads."

The group silenced.

"Father, we're tired. We want justice and closure. Will You give us that today? Help us find little Amy, no matter the outcome. Keep all these fine people safe and hold the weather off for us. Thank You. Amen."

Murmurs of amen filled the room.

The warden clapped again. "Okay, grab supplies and head out. Keep in constant contact. Each group has a sat phone."

Dr. Patch approached Violet. "We're in the same group which, of course, I requested as I'm in charge of whatever—" she pointed to Wolf "—he finds. I know Dr. Martin gave you leniency, but you won't get that from me. Let's head out." She knocked into Maverick on the way by before exiting the building.

"Wow. Who spit in her coffee this morning?" Jill asked. "I've heard she's ruthless, but seriously. I'm guessing she's on Santa's naughty list."

Maverick held the chuckle bubbling inside at Jill's funny comment. Now wasn't the time. They had a job to do. "Vi, let's gather food, water and a sat phone."

"I need to confer with Supervisor McGregor first. I'll meet you outside." Violet approached the bearded man.

An hour after Maverick gave Wolf the seek command, Dr. Patch's group, which also included Sara, Jill and Violet, turned down a trail, following the K-9 deep into the mountains. A question rose in Maverick's mind.

How many secrets did this trail hold? Secrets to how the Hancock family died and to where Amy now rested?

"Where is this dog leading us?" Dr. Patch's voice brought him out of the reverie into which his questions had led him.

He didn't care for the woman's tone. "He's trained to find human remains. We have to follow where his nose leads, and this weather can play havoc."

Dr. Patch stopped. "Violet, you trust a dog over your GPR device?"

"Right now, I trust Wolf not only with finding Amy, but with my life." Violet's firm voice proved she wasn't letting this woman take over.

Good for you, Vi.

"It's true, Dr. Patch," Jill said. "I've seen the dog in action."

Wolf barked and steered right onto a different path.

"He's caught a scent." Maverick pointed. "Let's go." He didn't wait for an answer, but followed his dog.

The group adjusted their course and plodded through the snow after Wolf.

Suddenly, he stopped before fleeing into the woods, off the path.

"Where's he going?" Violet asked.

"Whatever scent he caught is in the trees." Maverick parted the branches and trampled into the deep snow.

He stopped, searching the area.

"Where did he go?" Violet stood beside him.

"Good question." Maverick did a one-eighty, but when he couldn't spot his dog, trepidation tensed his muscles. He pointed to the tracks heading deeper into the woods. "This way, but first I need to hear from him. Wolf, speak!"

Seconds later, the dog barked.

Relief relaxed Maverick's shoulders. *Thank You, Lord.* With the threat on Wolf's life, Maverick had to keep his dog in his sight.

"This way." He hustled through the trees in search of his dog and whatever he had alerted to.

Maverick halted in his tracks.

Wolf sat next to a body lying in the snow.

But not Amy Hancock.

Violet peered over Maverick's shoulder. His loud intake of breath told her whatever Wolf had found wasn't good.

A male wearing a search vest lay half-buried in the snow, a rope nestled around his neck.

"Wait, I saw him in the crowd at the park station." Jill remained close to the trees, arms crossed.

Violet walked a wide circle around the man, then approached and kneeled, searching for a pulse. She sat back on her heels, her shoulders slumping. "He's gone, but is still warm."

"There you are. I lost you for a minute. Wait—" Sara paused when she saw the man in the snow.

"Sara, he's dead, but still warm." Violet lifted the rope with her gloved hand. "Murdered with this."

"Don't touch anything else." Her friend's hand flew to her sidearm. "Whoever did this could still be close. Did Wolf alert to anything other than the body?"

"No, but there are human tracks leading that way." Maverick pointed to the left.

Dr. Patch brushed by the group. "Let me check him."

"Wait, stay—"

Dr. Patch ignored Sara's order and dropped into the snow beside the deceased man. She removed her gloves and felt the body. "I'm not a medical examiner, but I would hazard a guess this person has been dead for at least an hour. The killer is probably long gone by now." She searched his pockets and passed his wallet to Violet. "Seems the killer left this behind."

Violet opened the leather folder. Hundred-dollar bills were still inside. "Definitely not a robbery."

Maverick gave Wolf a treat and reattached his leash.

"Someone must have killed him as soon as we started searching," Violet said. "Did anyone call in to report this person missing from their group?"

"You check in." Sara raised her weapon. "I'm going to search around for any sign of the killer. Maverick, have Wolf on guard." She turned to Dr. Patch. "Now that you've assured us the victim is deceased, please step away. This is an active crime scene."

Violet didn't miss the underlying tone in her friend's voice. Irritation laced her words. Clearly, Sara had trouble with the woman's unprofessional actions, too. "Mav, let's move back."

He nodded and commanded Wolf to do the same.

Violet fished out the sat phone and dialed the park warden's number.

"Warden Irving speaking."

"Hey, Doug. It's Violet. I wanted to apprise you of a situation here." She explained what Wolf had alerted to.

The man's sharp inhale revealed his shock. "Who is it?"

Violet extracted the man's driver's license. "Steven Nason. Has his group reported him missing?"

"Let me check. I'm searching with a group close to your location." The rustling of paper filtered through the phone. "Sorry I had to grab my clipboard. So far, only two groups have provided updates. No signs of anything suspicious. Nothing from Steven's group."

"We need to alert the others that there's a killer out there. Perhaps call off the search." Violet hated to suggest that, but a killer could still be in the forest.

"Wait, Steven was murdered?"

"Strangled with a rope. The ME will verify that, but that's what it looks like." Violet eyed Steven as sorrow hit her. She didn't know him. Did he have a family?

Maverick's radio blared out a message from a searcher. "Chuck from our group is missing. Lost contact an hour ago."

Violet's jaw dropped. "Doug, did you hear that?"

"Yes, what is going on? Chuck was in a different group than Steven."

The radio crackled again. "Our GPS was tampered with. We're way off course."

"Violet, I have to go. Something's happening to the teams. Is Constable Daley with you?"

"She just went to check our area for the suspect."

"I'll contact Everett and give the teams an update. Have Daley secure the scene. We'll get more constables to your location. Stay safe." He ended the call.

Violet stuffed the phone into the backpack.

"What's going on?" Maverick asked.

She gave him an update. "Mav, someone is sabotaging our search. That tells me one thing."

"What?"

"Amy Hancock is indeed somewhere in this part of the park and the killer is trying to stop us from finding her remains."

Sara returned moments later. "Just got a call from Everett. He's on his way here with the medical examiner."

"What's his ETA? We have to keep searching." Violet updated Sara with the situation and her suspicions. Even though she'd suggested canceling, she wanted their group to keep going.

"Everett just said that Warden Irving was going to call off the search." Sara grazed her arm. "I'm sorry. I know how much you want to help find Amy, but we can't risk any more lives."

"But I feel we're so close." Disappointment surged through Violet at the thought of having to vacate the park. "Can we keep going until it's official, Sara?"

"Not without me. I will not leave you unprotected."

"She won't be," Maverick said. "I'm here with Wolf."

"I realize that, but remember, Ragnovica is also targeting your dog." Sara checked her watch. "Everett will be here soon. We can head out then."

Snowflakes fluttered to the ground, increasing the angst

flowing through Violet. She checked the skies. Darkened clouds had moved in.

If whoever was sabotaging their search didn't stop them, the approaching storm would.

Come on, Nick. Get here. Fast.

Violet's shoulders slumped with relief when Constable Nick Everett brought backup and the medical examiner to the forest thirty minutes later. Time for the group to continue their search.

Time.

Something they didn't have with the pending storm and a killer in the forest. Warden Irving still hadn't called off the search.

In fact, Violet hadn't heard from him or any of the other groups at all. The saying "No news is good news" came to her mind, but in this case no news *wasn't* good, with someone threatening the search parties.

Violet approached Sara, who had finished speaking with the constables and medical examiner. "Can we continue?"

"Yes, I was just asking Everett to take over here. He's also going to consult with Warden Irving. I don't like it. We can't seem to get in touch with him. Something isn't right." She checked the skies. "And the snow is picking up. We have to move or we'll get stuck in the park, and we definitely don't want that. Dr. Patch, we're heading out. You coming?"

"Of course." She picked up her bag from the snowy ground and pointed to Wolf. "You gonna get him sniffing?"

The dog growled.

Violet smirked. This woman really knew how to get under everyone's skin. Including a dog's.

Maverick pursed his lips and unleashed his K-9. "Wolf, seek!"

Once again, the dog raised his snout in the air in different directions before barreling through the snow, heading north.

The group gathered their belongings and followed the K-9.

After twenty minutes of pursuing Wolf through trees and fighting the increasingly treacherous, snowy weather, Violet glanced behind her to ensure Jill, Sara and Dr. Patch were close.

Only a wall of white had followed her. "Maverick, stop." Violet's breath labored and her heart rate increased, sending her into a panicked state.

"What is it?" He commanded Wolf to halt.

"I don't see Sara and the others. They were just there." Violet yelled their names and retraced her steps, stumbling over an object stuck in the snow.

Jill's ground-penetrating radar device, but no sign of her or the others.

Had Ragnovica got to their search party, too?

"Where could they be?" Maverick wiped the snow off his jacket. How had the blizzard crept up on them so quickly? "Vi, stay close. I don't want you getting lost, too."

"I don't like this." Violet placed her hand on her chest.

Something wasn't right. Maverick grabbed her arm. "What's wrong?"

"My heart. Irregular beat. I'll be fine." She breathed in and out, vapors blending in with the snow. "It just has to subside."

Not good. "We need to head back down the—"

Wolf pranced around the duo, whining.

Maverick bent over and petted the dog's back. "What's up, boy?" He reattached the K-9's leash. Maverick wasn't about to lose sight of his dog, too.

Wolf barked and tugged Maverick forward.

"He's alerting to something. Maybe the others. We need to follow." He reached out to her. "Give me your hand. I can't risk us getting separated."

She complied, and together they let Wolf lead them forward.

Moments later, they stopped at the edge of a rickety bridge. "Wolf, halt."

The dog obeyed, but turned and barked.

"Whatever he's alerting to is across the bridge." Maverick surveyed their position to get his bearings. "You know this park. Where are we?"

The swing bridge connected one side of the trail to the other, with a river beneath it.

"We're at the northern tip of the Talber Path." She pointed. "Talber Mountain area is across the bridge. Do you think the others crossed here or were…" Her words trailed off.

"Don't think that way. This blizzard blasted in so fast, they may have gotten disorientated. Perhaps that's what Wolf senses. Not another body."

Wolf barked again and dragged Maverick toward the bridge.

"He's wanting to go across. Is it safe, Vi?"

"I haven't been on this side of the park for quite some time, but I think so."

Her tone didn't give Maverick much reassurance. "Should we risk crossing?"

She tipped her head toward Wolf. "He's telling us we do. I'm sure the park warden would have roped off the area if it wasn't safe. The bridge empties into a trail of caves that visitors often explore, especially this time of year."

Maverick sighed. "Okay, I'm trusting you and my dog. Let's take one step at a time. I'll go first." He placed one foot on the wooden bridge and pressed down.

It held. *So far, so good.*

He walked fully onto the bridge. The structure swayed but stayed secure. "It appears to be okay. We'll proceed slowly."

She nodded and, together, with Wolf leading them, the trio took baby steps as they crossed.

"Just a few more steps and—"

An explosion echoed throughout the mountainous region, followed by thunderous rumbles in the distance.

Wolf's bark level increased, warning them as the whumping sound grew louder.

"Avalanche!" Violet yelled from behind Maverick. "There's a cave just ahead, but we need to cross the bridge. Go!"

Even though Maverick couldn't see past the white blizzard wall, he guessed mounds of snow were collapsing quickly. They had to get to safety.

He didn't relish the thought of being buried alive.

FIFTEEN

Violet pushed Maverick into action, and they scurried across the bridge. She ignored her racing heart and concentrated on her bearings. *Lord, please help the cave entrance to be clear. We need a win.* Increased rumbles sounded to her right. Outrunning an avalanche wasn't how she expected her day to end. Also, how could she tell Maverick that she hated caves? Right now, the caves were their only hope.

Keep your ears in nature.

The last half of her father's motto bull-rushed her. *You've got this.* Dad and her sister Jayla had taught her everything she needed to know on how to survive in situations such as avalanches.

She just prayed the snow wouldn't bury them inside the cave and turn their place of refuge into an icy grave.

Wolf barked, thrusting her back to their situation.

"Where's the cave?" Maverick asked.

She snatched his hand, leading him to the right. "Over here." She prayed her memory of the area was correct. After all, she'd just confessed she hadn't been to this part of the park in a while.

Seconds later, she pointed. "There!"

They rushed through the snowy opening, narrowly missing the avalanche's path.

Violet fumbled for her flashlight in her backpack. When she found it, she hit the button and light illuminated the darkened cave. She shone it around. Ice crystals glistened in the beam, bringing the cave's ceiling to life.

Normally a beautiful scene, but not when they were taking shelter from a raging avalanche.

Rumbling sounded to her left, and she swung the light toward the entrance. Snow tumbled over, blocking their exit.

"No!" Violet dropped to her knees. The flashlight slipped from her hold and clattered on the icy ground. Caves horrified her, and now she was trapped inside one.

Maverick placed his hand on her shoulder. "It's gonna be okay. There has to be another way out of here, right?"

Get a grip, Vi. This is your park. Think.

She pushed herself up. "Yes, if my memory serves me correctly." She pointed. "There are tunnels that lead to another entrance on the other side of the mountain." She sat on a nearby boulder. "But I need to rest first. Can you try your sat phone?"

Maverick wiggled out of his backpack's straps and removed the device, hitting the talk button. "Nothing. The cave is interfering with the satellite signal. The other exit is our only way back down the mountain."

"If it's not blocked, too. That avalanche may have buried us."

Maverick sat beside her. "This wasn't an accident. Did you hear that explosion?"

"Someone purposely triggered the avalanche. To what, bury evidence or to stop the searchers from finding Amy's remains?"

"I would guess both, but it doesn't make sense. We get a tip Amy is in this part of the park, but yet someone is also trying to stop us from finding her?" Maverick stuffed the phone back into his backpack and brought out water.

Frustration knotted Violet's neck muscles. "I don't understand it either. And I still haven't found Baylee."

"I hate to ask this, but could she somehow be involved?"

Violet bolted off the rock, slipping on the icy surface. She held her arms out, balancing herself. "How can you say that? She's my sister and not involved."

"But you don't know her, Vi."

"She's a Hoyt. Hoyts are honest and help others." Violet refused to consider Baylee may be involved, but she had to face the facts. She plunked herself down again and buried her head in her hands. "You're right. I don't know her, but I can't imagine her being Ragnovica."

Maverick wrapped his arm around her, holding her close. "Sorry that I suggested it. If she's anything like you, she wouldn't hurt a fly."

Violet lifted her head, tears forming. "I just want to find Baylee. She's in danger. I can feel it."

"That twin thing?"

"Yes." A tear trickled down her face. "I'm sorry for yelling. My nerves are on edge and I just want this over. Why is God allowing such turmoil in my life?"

Maverick took off his gloves and wiped her tears. "I don't have the answers, Vi, but He's close and looking after us."

Wolf barked.

"See, Wolf agrees." Maverick chuckled. "I want to get back to Riley and give her the best Christmas I can. This will be her first one without Piper. That's gotta be hard for a five-year-old."

"Tell me about Piper. I sense there's something you're holding back about what happened."

He released her and stood. "That's because I made a lot of mistakes during that time of my life."

"Mav, I've made enough of my own. I won't judge you." Jesse entered her mind. *Yes, colossal mistakes.*

He plunked back down. "I fell hard for Piper quickly. She was different from the other women I had dated." He took another swig of water. "You see, after university, I played the field. I'm not proud of that."

"I remembered you dating quite a few of my classmates." She snickered. "They called you the heart crusher."

"What? Lots of the gals I dated at university broke up with me, claiming my heart was elsewhere."

"What do you mean?"

He turned back to her, his eyes shining in the dimly lit cave. "Don't you know?"

Violet held his gaze, her heart skipping a beat. Could he have had a crush on her like she did on him? No, not possible. "That part of my life is a bit of a blur." Half-truth.

"I see."

Disappointment sounded in Maverick's tone.

So be it. She wouldn't risk opening her heart again.

"Tell me more about Piper." She had to change the subject.

"We grew close quickly. I took her to meet my mother. My father had died a year before that." He hesitated before continuing. "Mom told me after that she sensed something was off with Piper, but I refused to believe her."

Violet harrumphed. She knew that feeling all too well.

"What?"

Oops. Keep your thoughts inside, Vi. "Nothing. Go on."

"I told you about our relationship, but not everything. This all happened before I surrendered my life to God." He stilled for a few seconds. "Piper and I moved in together. For about two months, I was happy, but then things changed."

"In what way?"

"She stayed out later, stating she was having dinner with her coworkers. I believed her until—"

"You caught her cheating?" Was that the part of the story he'd left out?

"Not exactly, but I suspected it and confronted her. She denied it. I believed her because I refused to acknowledge she would do that to me. I changed to keep her from leaving me. Tried to become the man I imagined she'd want." He fiddled with his water bottle. "It was after a few more months that my boss fired me. You know the rest."

She placed her hand over his. "I hate to ask this, but are you sure Riley is yours?"

"I did a paternity test. She's mine." He stood and fished out a treat, tossing it to Wolf. "I've held that information to myself for too long." He turned to face her. "I've been ashamed of the way I acted. No one should ever mold themselves into someone they're not just to earn love."

She raised her hands. "I've done some things I'm not proud of, too, so no judgment. I also made a terrible choice."

"Tell me."

She sat back beside him. "I met Jesse not long after I started working at Asterbine Park. He was the lead archeologist. I don't like to mix romance at the worksite, but he lured me in with his charm and compliments. When he asked me out for the first time, I couldn't resist, even though people around me warned me not to date him."

"Why would they do that?"

"They knew what he was really like." Violet withdrew her water bottle and drank, gathering her next words carefully. "To make a long story short, like you, I fell hard and fast."

"What happened?"

"I denied the signs. At first, it started with him joking to park employees about me, ridiculing me. Questioning my procedures, choice of friends, everything."

"How long did you date?"

"Eight months. After I introduced him to my friends, Sara challenged me about him right away. I refused to listen until..." She stopped. Could she continue?

Maverick took her hand. "You can tell me."

She inspected his kind eyes, expecting to see judgment, but only found concern. "Until he hit me. I walked away after that and broke it off. Unfortunately, he wouldn't take no for an answer and began stalking me."

"What?" Maverick clenched his fists.

"Yes. I took out a restraining order, but that didn't stop him." Violet placed her hand on her abdomen where he'd left his mark. "Not too many people are aware of this, but he followed me home one night and broke into my condo."

Maverick drew in a breath. "Did he—"

"No." She knew what he was thinking, as that scenario had entered her mind when he breached her property. She could see it in Jesse's eyes. "I tried to fight him off, but he stabbed me."

Anger flashed in Maverick's eyes. "What happened next?"

"I grabbed a frying pan and hit him over the head. It knocked him out. I called 911 before I fainted from the blood loss. I woke up in the hospital with my mother by my side."

"Did the police arrest him?"

"Yes, he's still serving time." She paused. "My mother started quoting Scripture to me, stating God has a reason for what happened. Not that I didn't believe that, but it wasn't what I needed to hear at the time. That was the night our relationship turned. I said some things to her I regret to this day."

"That's why I sensed a major tension between the two of you?"

Violet nodded. "And the news of her keeping Baylee a secret hasn't helped." Again, tears prickled the back of her eyelids. "I'm still ashamed of myself for not seeing through Jesse's supposed love for me."

"And you've carried the guilt ever since."

If only he knew the other guilt she carried, but that secret would remain buried like the snow that blocked the cave's entrance. If he discovered what she'd hidden from him, he'd never forgive her.

And right now, she couldn't handle that.

Maverick pushed a strand of hair off her face and tucked it behind her ear. "It's not your fault."

She stared into his eyes, which were full of compassion.

His gaze dropped to her mouth, and he inched closer.

Violet froze, waiting for his lips to touch hers. A kiss she had longed for years from Maverick Shaw. Even dreamed about. She closed her eyes, anticipating his kiss.

But it didn't come.

She opened her eyes to find Maverick had pulled away—his expression unreadable. "What's going—"

Wolf growled and barked.

"Well, isn't this cozy?" Santa Man emerged from a different tunnel inside the cave, holding a gun.

Maverick and Violet stood quickly.

Not only had Maverick rejected her, but now their lives were in danger.

Again.

***

Maverick's muscles tightened at the sight of Santa Man. How did he keep finding them?

"What? Surprised to see me?" The man entered the cavern. "I have too much at stake to let you both slip through my fingers. Ragnovica raised the bounties on your heads, and I need to get back into her good graces."

The mention of a female at the helm sent Maverick's mind raging. Who was Ragnovica? Could she be someone they knew? Someone right under their noses? That had to be the case, as it seemed they always found them easily.

Once again, Wolf growled, reminding Maverick that not only were their lives in jeopardy, but so was his dog's. He had to stall to think of a scenario to get them out of this mess. "How do you keep finding us?"

The man sneered. "You haven't figured that one out yet? I'm shocked. You won't make it out of this cave anyway, so I might as well tell you." He waved the gun at Violet's backpack. "Check behind her zipper in the front pocket."

Violet hesitated. "What are you talking about?"

"Check it!" His loud, irritated tone boomed in the cave.

She set her pack onto the rock and unzipped the front pocket, feeling inside. "There's nothing there."

"Behind the zipper. Ain't you listening?"

"Let me check." Maverick felt around the edge of the zipper. "There's a seam here." He pried it open and stuck his fingers inside, lifting out a round device. He held it up. "It's a Bluetooth tag."

"What?" Violet addressed the man. "How did you put it in there?"

"I didn't. Someone very close to you did." He threw his head back in laughter. "Someone you trust." He waved the Glock. "That was your first mistake."

"Who?" Violet asked. "Tell me, since you're going to kill us anyway."

"First, I need what you stole, Baylee." He harrumphed. "Well, you stole my heart, but you can't return that. It's broken. Hand it over."

"How many times do I have to tell you? Baylee is my sister. I'm Violet. You have the wrong twin."

Maverick guessed from Violet's heightened tone that she was on the brink of losing her cool. If they were to get out of this alive, he had to contain the situation, but how could Maverick get Wolf to attack the suspect without drawing attention?

His dog's focus shifted to Maverick, as if waiting for some type of command.

Wait! Maverick resisted the urge to snap his fingers. His other silent command. The one he had taught Wolf in case Maverick couldn't speak.

Like now.

But first he had to bide his time for the perfect moment. He couldn't put anyone at risk like he had at university. *Keep Santa Man distracted.* He just prayed it worked as he'd only tested it during training and not a real-life situation.

"Just tell us, man." Maverick shuffled closer to Wolf. "Who would betray Violet?"

"First, I want what she stole. Is it in your bag?"

"What do you think she has?"

"My journal. It contains private thoughts."

Maverick rolled his eyes. "You're lying. Your inner most feelings aren't enough to kill someone."

"They are if my off-the-book dealings are also included between the pages."

"Let me guess. Ragnovica wasn't aware of these dealings and now you don't want her to find out, so you need the journal." Maverick caught Violet's attention and tipped his chin toward the tunnel. He had to get her to move out of the way.

"You're smarter than you look, Dog Man."

"We know the crime lord is female, but who is Ragnovica?" Violet asked.

"You'd think I tell you if I knew? I'd be a dead man. She's kept her identity from all of us. Only Bobby, her closest bodyguard, knows."

"What dealings did you record in your journal?" Violet edged toward the tunnel.

"All my business deals over the years. My dad started an adoption agency, and I took over for him when he passed." He focused on Violet. "You really aren't Baylee, are you? You confronted me when you took the journal and knocked me out cold, so you would have known that."

Violet stopped moving. "Wait, did your father orchestrate my sister's kidnapping?"

"You mean adoption."

Instead of heading to the tunnel, Violet shifted her position toward the gunman, her eyes narrowing. "How can you say that? He worked with a doctor to pronounce my sister dead and then stole her from my mother!"

Not good. Violet's rage was taking over. Not that Maverick blamed her. This man's father had helped to kidnap her sister.

Santa Man aimed the Glock at Violet. "Stay there. If you're not Baylee, then you know where she is."

She raised her hands. "If I did, I wouldn't tell you, so go ahead. Kill me."

No, Violet. Don't antagonize the man.

Maverick had to distract him. "You can't tell me you work for Ragnovica but don't know who she is." He caught Violet's attention again and dipped his head toward the tunnel entrance, praying she'd listen this time.

"I've only ever contacted her online, but I have my suspicions about who she is." The man yanked zip ties out of his back pocket, tossing them at Violet. "Put these on your boyfriend."

It was now or never. Maverick had to act. *Lord, please help this to work.*

He snapped his fingers and flicked his hand toward Santa Man. His silent command.

Wolf sprang into action and barreled toward the suspect, leaping into the air. He latched on to his arm and knocked the gun to the ground.

The Glock skidded toward Maverick, and he scooped it up, aiming it at the assailant. "Stay still."

Wolf growled, keeping his hold on the man.

"Get this beast off me," he yelled.

"Not so tough now, are you?" Maverick inched forward. "Wolf, out."

Wolf retreated.

"Violet, tie him up with those." He pointed to the zip ties lying on the ground.

"My pleasure." After complying, she turned to Maverick. "Okay, now what?"

Maverick pointed to the tunnel. "He leads us out of here." He nudged Santa Man forward. "Get going. Don't try anything funny. Remember, my dog is right behind you."

The man spat. "Keep him away."

"I will if you obey. Now go."

After fifteen minutes of making their way through the tunnels, they emerged on the opposite side from where they had entered.

Maverick scanned the area. "Vi, where are we?"

She circled, checking her bearings. "We're on the south side of Talber Mountain."

Maverick kept the gun trained on their prisoner. "Grab the sat phone and get in touch with Sara. Explain what happened and where we are."

Violet called Sara and shared their location before ending their conversation. "She's close and should be here within thirty minutes."

Santa Man harrumphed. "You trust the cops?"

"You got something to say?" Maverick asked.

"My sources say Ragnovica is tied to the police department. How many women are on Asterbine Canyon's police force?"

Only one that Maverick knew about.

Constable Sara Daley.

And she was headed their way.

SIXTEEN

Violet searched the recesses of her mind for any sign of the man's insinuation that her friend, Constable Sara Daley, was Ragnovica, but she came up empty. Sara was a devout Christian and a good friend. One who had been there for Violet among countless troubles, including her messy breakup with Jesse. No way was Sara guilty.

Or was she an exceptional deceiver?

Violet clamped her eyes shut, attempting to silence the battle over Sara's loyalties going on in her head.

"Vi, you okay?" Maverick's question drew her out of her thoughts.

She opened her eyes. "I don't trust what he's saying. Sara wouldn't betray me, or anyone else for that matter. She's a cop."

"I don't know her like you, but I trust your judgment." He checked his watch. "She should be here soon. You called twenty minutes ago."

Violet leaned against the cave's entrance. "Yes, and she'll set him straight."

She had to, because Violet refused to believe anything else.

Fifteen minutes later, Wolf barked, alerting them to movement in the trees.

Maverick lifted the gun he still carried. "Who's there?"

Sara and Dr. Opal Patch emerged, but stopped at the sight of the weapon pointed at them.

"Whoa now, Maverick." Sara raised her hands. "Lower the gun."

"I will when you ease our minds." He addressed Violet, but kept his eyes trained on Sara. "Violet, I'll let you ask the question."

Sara's focus traveled from Maverick to Violet. "Vi, what's going on?"

Violet mustered the courage to confront her friend. She didn't want to consider Sara had betrayed her, but Violet had been wrong before about a loved one's allegiance.

She stomped into Sara's personal space. "Are you Ragnovica?"

Sara's mouth dropped open, then clamped shut as her lips flattened into a straight line.

But she remained silent.

Why? Could Violet be wrong about her best friend? Like she was with Jesse? "I'm waiting. Answer the question." Violet held her ground without flinching.

Sara's eyes narrowed. "How can you even ask me that with everything we've been through together?"

"That's exactly why I *have* to ask. You know what happened with Jesse." Violet pointed to Santa Man. "He says Ragnovica is connected somehow to the police department and you're the only female constable Asterbine Canyon Police Department has."

"And you're going to trust a criminal over your best friend? Vi, we've known each other for six years now."

Violet cringed on the inside, and she hated the accusation she'd thrown at her friend. "You still haven't answered the question."

"No! I'm not Ragnovica. I save lives. I don't take them." Sara averted her eyes and nudged Violet out of the way. "Maverick, please lower your weapon."

He complied. "She's telling the truth, Vi."

"How do you know? You barely know her." Something about Sara's demeanor raised a question in Violet's mind. Was her friend being totally truthful?

Maverick turned the weapon around and passed it to Sara with the handle toward her. "Because Wolf hasn't alerted to any type of danger with her. Not now or previously."

Sara took the gun and stuffed it at the back of her waistline. "At least he believes me, even if you don't."

"I feel you're holding something back."

Dr. Patch threw her hands up in the air. "Enough already. We need to head out. We're not getting any more searching done today with this weather, and I have work to do."

Leave it to the anthropologist to make it all about her.

Behind them, Santa Man chuckled.

Violet pivoted. "What are you laughing about?"

"Just love the tension between you all. Funny how a little doubt among friends can do that." He lifted his face to the sky. "But I'm cold and it's snowing harder. I'll take jail over these freezing temps. Can we go now?"

Sara marched up to the man. "You don't get to decide after the trouble you've sparked."

"Not to mention causing an avalanche," Maverick added. "But he's right. We need to get off the mountain."

The wind whipped through the trees, blowing snow from the branches as if confirming Maverick's statement.

Violet observed the weather. The earlier blizzard had eased a bit, but she didn't like the black clouds returning to the region. "First, I need to know something." Violet skirted around Sara and poked the man in the chest. "You haven't told us everything. How did you supposedly get Baylee to fall in love with you?"

He cocked his head, sneering. "What? My charm doesn't work on you?"

Violet shoved him backward. "Where is she?"

"No idea. She's hiding and has my property." He regained his balance and stormed toward her.

Wolf growled.

"He's not worth it, Vi." Sara's radio crackled, interrupting the conversation.

"Daley, ETA is five minutes to your location," Constable Everett said.

"Copy that." Sara turned to Violet. "Everett will escort our prisoner to the station and take Dr. Patch back to her vehicle."

"Wait, where's Jill?" Violet rubbed snow from her brow. "And how did we get separated from you? I looked back, and you were all gone."

"We thought Jill was with you. You had stepped through a cluster of trees. We followed, but we lost track of where you went, then the avalanche happened and we took cover." Sara placed her hand on Violet's sleeve. "Contrary to what you think, I care what happens to you and I'm happy to see you're okay. I was worried."

Violet searched her friend's eyes for any sign of deceit, but this time didn't find any. "I'm glad you're okay, too. Mav, show Sara what you found in my backpack."

He brought out the Bluetooth tags and motioned toward Santa Man. "This is how he's been tracking us, but he says someone close to us planted them. That's why we suspected you."

"He's wrong. It's someone else, but I have more news from Everett." Her eyes narrowed. "Or will you believe me?"

Violet frowned. "What is it?"

Sara nudged Violet out of Santa Man's earshot. "You remember that flash drive in the necklace? Digital forensics cracked it and found information on Asterbine Shipping. It's not concrete, but enough to suspect that the rumors of their illegal activities may be true. Our sergeant is requesting a warrant to search the premises." She held up her finger. "But one interesting bit of information is the location of a cabin they own right on the edge of your park near Hawkweed Mountain."

"What? That's not too far from here. We need to go search it before it gets dark." Violet put on her backpack. "We may find evidence if they own it. Maybe even some clues about where Amy was buried."

"We need to return to base. The storm is about to pick up. The park warden has now pulled everyone out of the park. Wait."

Sara approached Santa Man. "Did you kill that searcher and tamper with all our devices?"

"No. I've only been following Baylee. I mean Violet. Sure, I rigged explosives to collapse the snow, but that's all." He sneered. "That must have been Ragnovica. She's a cunning one and won't stop until you're all dead, including your twin, Violet." He glared at Wolf. "Even that beast."

Wolf growled.

Violet's heartbeat jack-hammered as a question rose.

How long before Ragnovica delivered on her promise to eliminate them all?

Maverick kept a tight hold on Wolf. He wasn't about to lose his friend and valuable weapon on the wintry mountain. Twenty-five minutes passed since they left Santa Man in Constable Everett's custody and took the path toward the abandoned cabin. Could Ragnovica be holding her secrets there? Secrets she would kill for? And more importantly—were they walking into a trap?

Sara, Violet and Maverick positioned themselves in a row to avoid getting separated, but Maverick wasn't sure how much longer before the path narrowed. They trudged through the fresh-fallen snow up an incline that leveled out into the wilderness.

"Vi, I don't understand why you believed I was guilty." Disappointment had replaced Sara's earlier angered tone.

Violet halted. "I know and I'm sorry, but you were acting oddly. Why?"

"I just had a heated conversation with my sergeant." She puffed out a breath. "He criticized my work on this case. Said I wasn't being objective because I was too close to you. He didn't trust in my abilities, so when you accused me, his words came back to haunt me. I couldn't believe you were doing the same thing."

Violet hugged her friend. "I'm sorry, but why didn't you just say that?"

Sara retreated from their quick embrace and adjusted her hat.

"I felt hurt and confused. And frankly, mad at you for believing a lie. Your actions surprised me, Vi."

"I'm sorry. I shouldn't have let that man get under my skin."

"I'm not like Jesse."

"I know that. Will you forgive me?"

The women hugged a second time.

Maverick's muscles twitched at the mention of Violet's ex-boyfriend-turned-stalker. It was a good thing the man was behind bars, because Maverick probably wouldn't be able to contain his anger. He'd hunt him down for hurting Violet. Thankfully, he could bury that anger about the past, but would he be able to still make things right with her regarding Angie's death?

Sure, they'd turned a corner with their conversation in the cave. He'd nearly kissed her. When she'd leaned toward him, Maverick couldn't remove the image of Angie's death, and his role in her demise, from his mind. Until they had a heart-to-heart about it, he wouldn't reveal his true feelings for her.

Emotions he'd felt since university, but denied.

She hadn't changed much since then. Her long, wavy brown curls were gathered at the nape of her neck, tumbling out from beneath her tuque and cascading down her back. Her rosy cheeks added to her cuteness and soft dimples always proved to be his downfall. He melted every time she smiled.

Maverick diverted his gaze, but couldn't deny his old feelings had returned.

And multiplied.

Maverick cleared his throat, attempting to curb his emotions. *Focus. You and Wolf have a job to do.*

"How close are we to the cabin?" Sara asked.

Violet looked left, then right. "Not exactly sure. This blizzard has complicated things."

Maverick drew Wolf closer. "Should we turn back? It's getting late."

"We can't! We've come this far." Violet dug out her paper map from her coat pocket and unfolded it. The edges flipped over in the blasting wind and she struggled to keep it flat.

"Let me help." Sara held one end.

"Okay, we came from here." Violet pointed.

Maverick leaned in for a better look. "There's the head of Talber Path where we entered twenty-five minutes ago. Do you remember how far the cabin is from that point?"

Violet placed her gloved index finger on the trail and traced it to the base of Hawkweed Mountain, which joined with Talber Mountain. "If my memory serves me correctly, it's right here." She tapped on the spot. "So, another five kilometers, which may take forever in this weather. It's also mostly uphill."

"And are we going in the right direction?"

Sara's elevated tone told Maverick she was nervous. Odd for a police officer. However, he understood. Getting turned around in a mountainous region could be dangerous and a blizzard complicated everything.

"Vi, you know how I hate to get lost," Sara added.

"We've got this." Violet pushed up her coat sleeve, revealing her smartwatch. She tapped on it. "We're heading north and that's what we want. Let's keep going. If we leave now, we should get there before dusk."

Maverick cringed. But then it would take them hours to return to the park's station, and he'd promised Riley to help her with puzzles.

And right now, Maverick had to keep his promises in order to stay in Riley's good books. She'd lost too much.

He eyed Violet. He also must earn her trust. How could he choose between the two? *God, help me do right by the females in my life.*

Maverick rolled his shoulders. He could do both. "Let's go. I hope the treacherous trek is worth it and we find something to help end this case."

Ninety minutes after getting lost twice because of the blinding conditions and slipping several times on the snowy path, the group entered a small clearing. The murky elements had blanketed the region with a heavy dusk.

Maverick removed his flashlight and turned it on. "Is that it? I can't see very well through the blizzard wall and the dusk. It took longer than we thought to—"

Wolf growled, then barked and lurched forward.

"What is it, boy?" Maverick shone the flashlight in the direction Wolf was facing.

And winced.

Several eyes glistened in the light's beam from the tree line.

A pack of wolves.

They emerged from the trees, the leader of the pack snarling and baring his teeth.

Maverick froze. Wolves were the one animal he feared the most, and now they surrounded them.

SEVENTEEN

Chilled prickles crawled up Maverick's spine as a crushing weight squeezed his heart, sending a jolt of adrenaline through him. He flashed back to when he was seven and surrounded by another pack of wolves. Even after all these years, the animals in front of him still had the same effect as they did back then. He stole a peek at the others to ensure they were okay. Violet remained as still as a statue. Sara's hand rested on her sidearm.

One wolf probably wouldn't attack a human, but a pack might. Maverick wouldn't take the risk of that happening. He glanced down at his K-9, who was looking at his handler as if waiting for a command. Maverick searched his memory for what his Scout leader had taught him all those years ago. The man had told his troop to not panic if they ever came up against a pack of wolves. He turned to Violet and Sara. "Keep eye contact with the wolves and don't run away. Make lots of noise."

They nodded.

The women yelled and waved their arms in the air, keeping their focus on the wolves.

Beside them, Wolf growled.

Maverick joined in the noise, but kept a tight hold on Wolf.

The dog barked ferociously, baring his teeth as if claiming the group of humans as his own, and for the wolves to leave them alone.

"Everyone, back away slowly." Maverick took one step backward, but kept his eyes focused on the leader of the pack.

The animal howled before bolting back into the forest. The others followed.

Violet let out an audible breath. "That was close."

"Too close," Sara added.

"Stay diligent." Maverick shone his flashlight toward the trees. Dusk had descended on them quickly. "They may have retreated, but they're probably still lurking. We need to get to the cabin and take refuge there." He reached down and ruffled Wolf's fur. "Good boy for protecting us. That brought back fears from my past I thought I'd buried."

"What do you mean?" Violet removed her flashlight and turned it on.

"I was seven and went camping with our Scout troop. We were having a blast, telling stories around the campfire. Laughing, singing songs, roasting marshmallows. You know, all the fun things boys do together." He paused. "Suddenly, a pack of wolves surrounded us. The leader jumped up and tried to scare them off. But he got too close and one bit him. I remembered what he taught us to do and had the others grab sticks. We made lots of noise. I hit the wolf who attacked our leader over the head to scare him away, but I still got bit. That experience instilled a fear of wolves in me."

"I'm proud of you for facing your fear and saving us. I totally forgot everything my father taught me." Violet's lips pursed.

"I'm a cop and should know better," Sara said.

"Well, I totally understand. I hesitated before my Scout lessons came back to mind." He scanned the trees. "Looks like they're gone. Let's continue toward the cabin."

"Wait. If you're scared of wolves, why did you name your dog Wolf?" Violet asked.

"I didn't." Maverick petted his dog. "Austin did. After I told him my story, he said the name was appropriate and an excellent reminder to face our fears constantly. In his words, 'Facing your fears head-on is the only way to truly defeat them.' Today was the day I did that, but almost turned around and ran."

"But you didn't." Violet smiled. "That's sound advice from Austin."

Maverick squatted in front of Wolf. "Plus, we bonded immediately, didn't we, boy?"

The dog barked and nestled into Maverick's hold.

Sara clapped. "Okay, time to go. I want to get off this mountain."

They continued toward the cabin and, ten minutes later, stopped at the edge of a clearing.

A small, dilapidated cabin lay nestled among pine and spruce trees a few feet from their location. A plume of smoke rose from the chimney as a light flickered in the window, which meant two things.

The cabin wasn't abandoned, and they weren't alone.

Sara drew her weapon. "Okay, my turn to take over. Stay back. We don't know who's behind that cabin door. For all we know, it may be Ragnovica herself. We trust no one, understood?"

"Understood," Maverick and Violet said together.

Maverick tugged on Wolf's leash. "Wolf, protect."

Even in the dimmed light, Maverick noted his dog launch into a protective stance, standing as tall as possible on all fours.

"Let's go." Sara lifted her gun and flashlight simultaneously, plodding through the snow toward the cabin.

The pack of wolves howled in the distance, reminding Maverick they were still nearby. It was as if they were signaling this place was their territory. *You can have it back soon.*

Wolf growled.

Sara inched her way up the snow-covered wooden steps and placed herself to the door's right. "Maverick, take Wolf and stand to the left," she whispered.

He complied. "Vi, stay behind me."

She nodded, hovering close.

Sara pounded on the door. "Police, open up."

The light flicked out.

When no one answered, Sara placed her hand on the doorknob and turned. "Police, coming in." She pushed the door open, keeping her flashlight and weapon trained on whoever was lurking in the cabin.

Wolf's growl elevated Maverick's pulse.

The group trampled inside out of the icy winds.

A figure stood in front of the fire, her face glowing and reminding Maverick of a spooky movie.

Sara's flashlight beam settled on the person.

Maverick sucked in a breath.

Violet stared back at him. Impossible. Violet was behind him.

"Baylee?" Violet's hushed question revealed her shock.

But Wolf's growl continued to send shivers of panic jolting through Maverick's body along with a question.

Could Violet's twin be Ragnovica?

Violet's jaw dropped in disbelief as her own image stared back at her without a mirror. "I can't believe it's you." She ignored her shaky limbs and sauntered around Maverick.

Wolf snarled a low growl.

Maverick grasped Violet's arm, yanking her backward. "Wait, she may be armed."

"She's not."

"Then why is my dog agitated, Vi?"

Sara stepped in front of Violet. "He's right. She may be Ragnovica."

Baylee rolled her eyes. "Hardly. Why would I be emailing you if I'm that criminal queen?" She took a step.

Sara raised her weapon. "Stay there."

Violet's twin halted, lifting her hands. "Please. I'm not, but you may have led her here."

"Maverick, close the door. I'll check her for weapons." Sara passed her flashlight to Violet. "Shine it on her."

Maverick closed the door, shutting out the fierce wind and blizzard.

"Really?" Violet sighed, but did what she was told. "This is ridiculous."

"I'm just being cautious. Remember, it's my job." Sara kept her weapon trained on Baylee and frisked her with her left hand. "She's clean."

"Of course she is." Violet rushed to her sister and threw her arms around her. "I'm so glad to meet you." She didn't want to let go for fear of losing her again.

"Can't breathe." Baylee's whispered words boomed in Violet's ear.

Violet released her sister. "Sorry, I'm just happy to find you." She gestured toward the others. "This is Constable Sara Daley and K-9 handler Maverick Shaw, and his dog, Wolf."

Maverick relit the oil lantern. "Why have you been hiding, Baylee?"

The glow from the lantern flickered on the log walls, reminding Violet why they had come to the cabin. "And why are you here?"

Baylee pointed to the chairs. "How about we sit first?"

Maverick positioned himself and Wolf beside the fireplace. "I'll stand, thank you."

"Suit yourself." Baylee plunked onto the couch.

Violet glared at Maverick before sitting beside her sister and taking her hand in hers. "I'm sorry. We're just on edge, as wolves almost attacked us."

"And don't forget almost being buried by a man-made avalanche," Maverick added.

"Right." Violet studied her sister's pretty face. They were identical twins except Baylee's hair was shoulder-length, while Violet's trailed farther down her back. "We would have gotten into so much mischief as kids. We could have fooled everyone. No wonder the tattooed Santa Man thought I was you."

Her eyes narrowed. "You mean Walt Dale. One of Ragnovica's many henchmen."

Sara holstered her weapon and sat across from them. "So that's his name. He burned off his fingerprints, so in the short time we had him in custody, we couldn't ID him. Answer the question. Why are you hiding here?"

"That's a long story. I'll give you the abridged version." Baylee leaned forward and rested her elbows on her knees, clasping her hands together. "I'm an investigative reporter and caught wind of an illegal adoption ring in my area. That investigation lead me here to Asterbine Shipping."

"Wait, where do you live?" Violet asked.

"British Columbia." Baylee stood and picked up a log and added it to the fire. "This may sound odd, but I always had this strange sense that I had siblings." She turned to Violet. "What about you?"

"We have lots of brothers and sisters, Baylee." Violet couldn't wait to introduce her to them. "But you're right. I've always felt something was missing in my life. Once I found out about you, I realized it must have been that twin-like intuition. How did you find out about me?"

"After my parents passed—my adoptive ones, that is—I found a birth certificate that was confusing to me. It listed my parents as unknown."

"And your parents never said you were adopted?" Maverick air-quoted the word *adopted*.

"Exactly. I was intrigued and started looking into it, checking county records. That sort of thing. I'm good at digging up information."

"When was this?" Sara asked.

"Six months ago. Through some reliable sources, I tracked down my original birth certificate. Or should I say, death certificate?" She sat back down. "At that point, I didn't know about my twin, but in short, I discovered others like me were sold to wealthy couples."

"And Walt's father was the one who started the agency," Violet added. "That much he told me, and he took over the business."

"Correct, Walter Dale Sr. He passed six months ago. Walt Jr. closed the agency there and moved it here." Baylee bit her lip. "So I came, too. I wanted to not only find my biological parents, but bring this agency to justice."

"What does this all have to do with Asterbine Shipping and Ragnovica?" Maverick set his gloves on the mantel.

Baylee stood again and walked to the small kitchen area. She reached into a cupboard and withdrew a book, holding it up. "Walt kept extensive records among his personal diary."

Violet shot to her feet. "That's what he thought I had. He told us he loved you and you betrayed him."

Baylee sat back on the couch and passed the journal to Violet. "I hated to deceive him, but it was necessary in order to find out the truth." She addressed Maverick. "To answer your question. Walt now runs his business through the shipping containers at Asterbine. I did some sleuthing there when I pretended to be a marketing consultant to help improve their social media platform."

Sara whistled. "Wow, you are resourceful, but why didn't you come to us when you discovered all this?"

"Because Ragnovica found out my real identity and I wasn't about to stick around. I heard about the Hancock murders through the news." She turned to Violet. "And I saw you on television. I was shocked to be staring at myself in the mirror."

Violet leafed through the entries. Personal thoughts were intermixed along with the ledger accounts of stolen babies sold through his agency. "When was this?"

"A few days ago when I first emailed you. I got your email through the park's website." She glanced back at Sara. "I hid in a few different places before coming here to the cabin yesterday. I had discovered Asterbine owned it and figured they may have hid information here."

"Did you find anything?" Violet handed the book to Sara. "You'll want to add this to your evidence against Asterbine."

"No, it appears like they abandoned it." Baylee fiddled with the tassels on her sweatshirt.

Violet's sister was holding something back. "What aren't you telling us, Baylee?"

She looked up. "What do you mean?"

"Even though we just met, I feel like I know you, and you're acting the same way I would if I was hiding information." Violet reached over and squeezed her hand. "You can trust us."

Baylee sprang upright. "Can I? I've discovered that Ragnovica's connections run deep. She's already tried to kill me once."

Violet gasped. "When?"

"A week ago. That's why I left the shipping company abruptly and went into hiding."

"But why hide in a spot they own?" Maverick asked.

Baylee shrugged. "I figured it was as good a place as any. Hiding right under their noses. Too obvious. Besides, once I got here, I knew I was safe because it appeared like the cabin had been abandoned."

"So tell us then what you're hiding." Maverick unleashed Wolf. "I trust Violet's judgment on her reading your body language."

Baylee's attention switched from him to Sara, back to Violet. "Fine." She dug into her back pocket and held up a flash drive. "This is what I found on Asterbine and should help you bring them down. And before you ask, I didn't contact the police earlier as I had planned to write an article exposing them. I know, that was wrong of me." She passed it to Sara.

Sara frowned and tucked the drive into her coat pocket. "What's on it?"

"I discovered over the past couple of months that the Hancock family cold case was just the beginning of Ragnovica's conspiracy. Asterbine Shipping is a front for various illegal dealings. Human trafficking, drugs, money laundering, illegal adoptions and lots more. You'll find everything on that. I was about to break the case wide-open when Ragnovica tried to kill me, or at least her henchman did."

"We've been looking into the shipping company closely as we heard the rumors," Sara said. "So far, we've only determined that it's owned by Carson Emerson. He's known for his harsh ways, but we haven't been able to gather evidence, so this will help."

"Do you know who Ragnovica is, sis?" *Sis* just slipped out, but seemed like a natural nickname for Violet to give Baylee.

"That's the one thing that still has me stumped. No idea, but whoever she is, she's taking over the business. I met no females while I was at Asterbine."

"How do you know she tried to kill you, then?" Sara asked.

"Because her bodyguard said she sent him to kill me, but I managed to escape."

Wolf suddenly hopped up onto all fours and paced the room, whining.

Violet stood. "What's wrong with Wolf?"

"I'm not sure. What is it, boy?" Maverick followed Wolf around the room until the dog settled beside the old wooden stove. "I think he might be alerting to something. Wolf, seek."

The dog retraced his steps, sniffing in different spots, but returned to the area around the stove. He stopped and clawed at the floorboards, barking.

Violet, Baylee and Sara all huddled around Wolf.

"There's something under there." Maverick lifted the poker from its stand and tried to pry apart the wooden planks.

One end of the board lifted. "Violet, can you help me? I'll pry using the poker, and you lift the board off."

She kneeled beside him. "Ready."

Maverick stuck the poker's sharp end into the crack and jimmied with more force.

The board popped upward, and Violet lifted it off, tossing it to the side. She peered into the opening. The dim lighting revealed fabric stuffed inside. "Sara, hand me your flashlight. There's something down there."

Sara turned it back on and passed it to her.

Violet aimed the beam into the hole, her breath catching.

Skeletal remains lay nestled among faded, frayed pink fabric.

This had to be the missing Amy Hancock.

Maverick tore off another floorboard, making the hole bigger. "Hand me the light, Vi."

She passed the flashlight to him.

He shone it around the skeleton, wrapped in what he guessed was a pink blanket. "Definitely appears to be a child." He turned back to the group. "Do you think this could be Amy Hancock?"

"That's my guess." Violet pointed. "Wait, what's that?"

A tarnished chain lay nestled among the remains.

"Looks like a necklace." Maverick fished a tissue out of his pocket and removed the item, holding it up. "It's a locket." He turned the pendant over and shone the light onto the back. "Wait, there's an engraving. 'Merry Christmas, Amy. Love, Mom and Dad XO.'"

Behind him, the trio let out a cry.

"It's Amy Hancock." Violet exploded to her feet. "Sara, we need to get the team here to extract the remains."

"I don't understand why she's buried here and not in the park like the others." Sara scratched her forehead.

"Very good question." Maverick wrapped the locket in the tissue and handed it to Sara. "You'll want this for evidence."

She pocketed the necklace and hit her radio button. "Dispatch, come in."

The radio squawked, but no reply came.

"Great. Maverick, do you still have that sat phone?" Sara held out her hand.

"Yes." He fished the phone out of his bag and passed the device to her. "It's not always reliable either, and this weather may not help."

Wolf once again growled.

Movement sounded on the roof.

"What is that?" Baylee asked.

"It's definitely not Santa and his reindeer." Maverick looked out the window, but total darkness had descended.

Something clattered down the chimney and landed in the fire.

Wolf barked.

"Get down!" Maverick sprang back to Violet and knocked her to the floor, covering her with his body. *Lord, protect us.*

The fireplace exploded, emitting gas into the cabin.

Someone was trying to smoke them out.

EIGHTEEN

"Someone found us and that was some type of gas bomb. Cover your noses." Maverick pulled his scarf over his mouth and blasted to his feet. He sprang to the door, but found it locked. "It's locked. How is it possible to be locked in from the outside?"

Sara also tried the door. "They must have somehow jammed the lock." She turned to Baylee. "Is there a back door?"

Baylee coughed and shook her head.

"There has to be a way out." Maverick quickly inspected the cabin.

Wolf barked and trotted to where Amy was buried, scratching beside the hole they'd created.

"What is it, Wolf?" Maverick kept his mouth covered and approached the hole. He shone the flashlight beyond Amy's remains. "Wait, the cabin is built on stilts without a foundation. We'll have to dig our way out. Sorry, Vi, but I have to move the skeleton. Our lives trump the evidence."

"Agreed." Sara kneeled beside him and shone the light inside. "It's a tight space. I'm the smallest of us. I'll crawl out and unjam the lock."

Maverick pried off another large piece of floorboard and carefully lifted out the remains from the hole, setting them aside. "Go. Take Wolf with you. There will be snow piled once you get to the edge of the cabin. He can dig faster than any of us." He pointed to the hole. "Wolf, down."

The dog jumped into the opening.

Sara crawled inside and followed Wolf, quickly disappearing.

The group left in the cabin coughed simultaneously.

Maverick's head spun as spots flickered in his vision. *Lord, help them get to the entrance and save us!*

Finally, after a few minutes, the door burst open. Sara appeared with her weapon drawn. "Quickly, get out!"

Baylee nabbed the journal sitting on the table and fled the cabin.

Maverick snatched his gloves from the mantel and held Violet's hand, whisking her outside.

They dropped to their knees in the snow, coughing and wheezing in breaths.

Wolf snuggled beside Maverick, licking his face.

"Thank you for saving us, boy." Maverick hugged his dog. "You're amazing."

Wolf barked.

"I'm going to check the perimeter and call Dispatch. I've left the door and windows open to clear out the cabin. Forensics will need to get here, along with Dr. Patch. Thankfully, the blizzard has lessened, but we're in for a bit of a wait." Sara pointed to the tree. "Go over there and stay hidden until you hear from me. Something tells me we're not alone."

Maverick agreed. It wasn't only the wolves lurking.

But someone more menacing.

Violet turned to Baylee as they approached the ranch's front door three hours later. "I forgot to tell you in all the excitement, but Mom is here. She doesn't realize I found you."

Baylee stopped midstep. "I'm not sure if I can do this. What if she blames me?" Her voice quivered.

"Why would she blame *you*? Trust me, she will be so excited to meet you." Violet opened the door and proceeded inside. "Welcome to Hawkweed River Ranch. You'll love it here. Maverick is moving us to one of the cabins on the ranch so we can be together. We have lots of sister time to catch up on."

Maverick had called Buck from his SUV and arranged for

everything. Since Erica Hoyt came, all rooms on the ranch were full, and Maverick had suggested the idea.

Violet agreed. She finally felt like this case was over and they were safe—all in time for Christmas. With the evidence Baylee had provided, the judge wouldn't be able to turn down getting a warrant. It was only a matter of time before Ragnovica—whoever she turned out to be—was arrested.

Violet had tried to get a hold of Jill, but she was still missing. Sara had the police checking her home. Dr. Patch had arrived at the cabin in record time. How she managed that eluded Violet, especially in the dark. Had she been lurking nearby? She had refused to wait until daylight. Of course, she chastised them for moving the remains, even though they explained why they had to. Seemed their escape wasn't as important to her as the condition of Amy's bones. Violet still wondered why Amy had been buried in the cabin.

The pitter-patter of tiny feet drew Violet's attention.

Riley entered the foyer and skidded to a stop, looking from Violet to Baylee. "You look the same."

Violet chuckled. "Riley, this is my twin sister, Baylee. Baylee, this is Riley. Maverick's daughter."

Baylee raised a brow but squatted and held out her hand. "Nice to meet you."

Riley placed her small hand into Baylee's. "What's a twin?"

"Two people who are born in the same womb," Baylee said.

Riley scrunched up her nose, revealing her confusion.

"Baylee and I were in my mommy's tummy together."

The redhead's mouth formed an O and she giggled.

Pounding footfalls sounded. "Violet, you're home—" Erica Hoyt halted and her mouth hung open. "Baylee." Tears glistened.

"Mom, we found her," Violet said. "Isn't she beautiful?"

"Yes." Their mother's faint reply squeaked out before she rushed forward, pulling Baylee into her arms. "I'm so sorry I let you go."

Baylee retreated from her hold. "It wasn't your fault. You believed the lie that I was dead."

Violet shrugged out of her coat and hung it on the wall hook. "Baylee, I officially want to introduce you to your mother, Erica Hoyt."

"This is the best Christmas present ever." Once again, their mother hugged her other daughter.

"Mom, let's video with the family," Violet said. "We can't waste another minute. Yes, it's fairly late, but they'll want to meet their sister, and Dad—his daughter."

The front door opened and Maverick entered with Wolf at his heels. "I see you've met. Your cabin is ready for you both to move in. Buck and his men have rechecked and secured the premises. Just in case."

"Thanks, Mav." Violet grazed his arm. "We're going to have a video call with the family first."

"Sounds good. How about I brew some decaf coffee after I build a puzzle with this little girl?" He lifted Riley and twirled her around.

She squealed, holding Maverick tightly.

The father-daughter moment melted Violet's heart and there was nothing more she wanted than to be a part of this little family.

If only he felt the same as she did.

Maverick sipped his coffee at the kitchen island an hour later, rehashing the day's events in his mind. Even though the police were confident that arrests were imminent, he still wasn't sure the danger had passed. He hated that Violet wouldn't be staying in the house, but realized she wanted to be close to her sister. Plus, right now, they required bonding time more than anything.

Violet had promised him she'd call at the first sight of any type of danger and assured him police were still patrolling outside the ranch's property.

"Hey, you. You're still up? Sorry, our conversation went a

little long." Violet shuffled into the kitchen and set her coffee cup into the sink.

"Yah, trying to unwind after today. How did the video call go?"

"Great. Everyone is so excited and can't wait to meet Baylee in person. Mom is making lots of plans."

"That's awesome. Here's the code for the back door, since the cabin is behind the ranch. Easier access for you." He handed her a piece of paper. "Where's Baylee?"

"Upstairs. We're heading to the cabin in a few minutes. I found some extra pajamas for her in my bag." Violet sat on one of the island's barstools. "You okay? You seem pensive."

"Just lots on my mind. Tomorrow is Christmas Eve and I still have lots of wrapping to do for Riley." He sipped his coffee. "I kind of went a little bananas and bought too much. I just want this Christmas to be special."

"It will be. She's warming up to you."

"Yes, and I don't want to do anything to blow it."

"Trust me. You will, as all parents do, but she'll forgive you."

Maverick rubbed her arm. "Does that mean you've forgiven your mother for not telling you about your twin?"

"I'm getting there."

"What about God?"

Violet recoiled and hopped off the stool. "Now you sound like my mother."

"Sorry, but He's given you such a beautiful gift with Baylee."

"And I should be grateful. Is that what you're saying?"

Maverick finished his coffee and took it to the sink. "Not in so many words, but I guess so. Grateful is how I'm feeling right now. Except..." He let what he really wanted to say trail off. Was now the time to talk to her about Angie's death?

"Except what, Mav? Come on, spit it out."

He took her hand and lead her back to the stool. "Please sit. I need to get something off my chest. It's been eating at me for years."

"You mean Angie?" She sat.

"Yes." He took the stool beside her and swiveled to face her, their knees touching. He forced his feelings for her aside and marshaled the courage to share his heart. "Sorry I acted so reckless that day. I was trying to be a hero."

She caressed his face. "You already were—and are—my hero. Mav, Angie's death isn't your fault. If anyone's, it's mine."

"What do you mean? You're not to be blamed."

Violet dropped her hands into her lap. "I feel guilty for surviving that day. It should have been me who got shot, not Angie."

"Why would you say that?"

She fiddled with her fingernails. "There's something I never told you."

He placed his hands on top of hers. "What are you talking about?"

"I knew the shooter. Well, not really, but I met him a few times before the shooting." She paused. "I saw him looking at weaponry in a book at the library."

Maverick bolted off the stool. "What? And you said nothing? Why?"

"I thought he was researching for an assignment, but when I saw him doing it again, I asked him point-blank."

"What did he say?"

"He shared how he was having a hard time with his mother's death and then discovered his girlfriend was cheating on him with someone at the university. He begged me not to say anything to anyone on the campus and I promised I wouldn't if he didn't take any action. He agreed. I believed him and felt sorry for him." She hung her head. "But my conscience wouldn't let it go, and I didn't feel talking to the police would break my promise, so I went to the police station. They thanked me and said they'd look into it. That was the day before Angie's death."

Maverick clenched his hands into fists. "You knew I blamed myself for her death and never said anything?" Maverick hated the angry words spieling out of his mouth, but he couldn't help it.

Tears spilled down her cheeks. "I'm sorry. I was ashamed. Still am. I should have said something to you, but then our friendship ended and we lost touch."

He raised his hands. "I will forgive you, Vi, but right now, I can't be near you. See you in the morning."

Maverick marched from the room, resisting the urge to turn back and wipe away her tears.

That would have to wait. He didn't trust the anger raging inside him.

Violet couldn't stop the flow of tears coursing down her cheeks. She fled the kitchen after Maverick's harsh reaction and had ran all the way to the cabin. Not that she blamed him. She was wrong for keeping that information from him. A mistake she'd never let happen again. She'd paid the ultimate price.

A friend's life and now any possible relationship with Maverick.

The man she knew in her heart she loved. No sense denying it any longer.

Baylee entered the bedroom and sat beside Violet on her bed. "What's wrong?"

"I'm a fool." Violet sniffed and rubbed her nose.

"Does this have to do with Maverick?"

"How did you guess?"

Baylee snatched a tissue from the box on the nightstand in between the two queen-size beds and passed it to her. "I see the way you look at each other. I've only known you for what—" she checked her watch "—six hours, but I've been in love before, so I know the signs. Plus, I'm your older sister. By two minutes. Spill."

Violet chuckled and blew her nose before unloading everything to her sister about Angie. The shooter. And Maverick.

Baylee took Violet's hand. "Sis, you need to stop blaming yourself. You've obviously carried this load for years. Time to put it in the past." She blew out a breath. "I should talk. I've made many mistakes in my life, but Maverick will forgive you."

"Will he? You didn't see the tortured look on his face."

"He will." Baylee hugged Violet before climbing under the plaid comforter of her own bed. "Right now, I need sleep."

"I understand. Baylee, I'm so glad we found each other."

A tear flowed down her twin's face. "Me, too. Thank you for introducing me to everyone. I can't wait to meet them all in person."

"They're gonna love you like I do."

"Already?"

Violet chuckled. "Already." She turned off the lamp.

"Vi, don't waste another minute. Tell Maverick how you feel about him."

Should she?

Violet yanked the covers close to her neck and sighed.

Yes, tomorrow she would make everything right and tell Maverick her true feelings.

Even if it meant his rejection.

NINETEEN

Hammering thrashed in Violet's ears and she struggled to open her eyes. She rubbed her head. Why did it hurt so much? *Come on, Violet, wake up.* She blinked open her eyes, squinting to clear the fogginess that had settled in her head. She wasn't prone to headaches, so why now? Violet leaned on her elbows and waited for the spinning to stop before fully sitting. Darkness still enveloped the room. The clock radio displayed 5:50 a.m.

Violet snatched her cell phone from the nightstand, swiping the screen to bring it to life. The glow illuminated the room, casting a flare of light onto Baylee's bed. Violet expected to see her sister sleeping.

Instead, her comforter lay rumpled, her bed empty.

"Baylee? You up already?"

The small cabin remained silent.

Violet flung off the covers and shot out of bed. Her heavy head continued to pound, and she swayed. She grabbed the headboard to steady herself.

Once she regained her balance, she wobbled to the bathroom and flicked on the light. Empty. "Baylee, where are you?"

She walked into the main living area and turned on the ceiling light. It, too, remained empty.

Had Baylee gone to the main house for coffee? But why when they had a K-cup machine here in the cabin?

Violet had to check. She floundered back to the bedroom and hastily dressed in a sweatshirt and jeans. It was then she noted Baylee's cell phone on the floor. Cracked with a text message on the screen.

Violet picked it up and read.

You deceived us, and now you'll pay. We have kidnapped your sister, and we will sell her to the highest bidder. We didn't want you. You need to suffer for what you've done. Don't try to save her or tell anyone. My spies will know. If I see you at the compound, Violet dies. R

Violet's breath hitched. They'd taken the wrong twin.

Her head pounded not only from whatever had caused her to feel dizzy, but from the fact she'd found her sister only to lose her.

Again.

Think, Violet.

Obviously, Ragnovica had taken Baylee to Asterbine Shipping. It was the only thing that made sense. And they were going to sell her into a human trafficking ring.

It was up to Violet to save her, but how, when Ragnovica had spies everywhere?

First, she had to get a vehicle. She snatched her coat and put on her boots before dashing out the door.

Violet slugged through the snow as quickly as possible and scurried up the backyard steps. She punched in the code Maverick had given her and eased the door open. *Lord, help everyone to still be sleeping. I need to get to Baylee.* Would God listen to her silent prayer?

She tiptoed to the utility room, where Buck kept the keys to their vehicles, and snagged the Jeep's key fob.

Claws clicking on the hardwood sounded. She froze. Wolf. Could she greet him without him barking? What was the command Maverick had given him to stay silent?

Wolf entered the room and rubbed against her legs.

She squatted in front of him. "Hey, boy," she whispered. The command entered her mind. "Wolf, silent."

The dog cocked his head but obeyed.

"Good boy." She rubbed his neck and grazed his collar.

An idea formed, and she straightened. "Wolf, come." She exited the room and crept into the kitchen with Wolf at her heels.

She snatched a pen and notepad, scribbling a hasty note to Maverick. She ripped it off and rolled it into a tube.

Violet squatted in front of Wolf and wrapped the note around his collar, kissing him on the forehead. "I'm counting on you, boy. Please take this to Maverick."

She stood. "Wolf, stay." Violet sauntered across the kitchen floor and turned.

Wolf heeded her instructions, but the sad look on his face made Violet think he knew exactly what she was doing.

Heading into danger.

Lord, please help Maverick find my note. And please be with Mom. She'll need your comfort.

Violet zoomed outside into the darkness, tears streaming down her face. Would she see her loved ones again?

She still had to tell Maverick how she felt, but now doubted she'd ever get the opportunity.

Wolf licked Maverick's face, bringing him out of a deep sleep. "What's going on, boy?" Maverick sat up and rubbed his dog's fur, glancing at the clock. 7:00 a.m. Ugh! He'd overslept, and now his dog wanted to be fed. Maverick threw off his covers and dressed in jeans and a plaid shirt. "Wolf, come."

Maverick silently passed Riley's and Erica's rooms, making his way down the stairs into the kitchen with Wolf following him.

Maverick withdrew the dog food and filled the bowl before adding water to the other one.

But Wolf barked and didn't eat.

Odd.

"Come on, boy. You must be starving. Eat."

The dog pranced around the kitchen, whining.

Buck entered the room. "Morning." He stopped and pointed. "What's up with Wolf?"

"I'm not sure. He's acting strangely. He always eats as soon as I fill his dish."

Wolf barked and plowed into Maverick's legs as if wanting to knock him over. Why?

Maverick kneeled in front of his dog. "What's gotten into you?" He rubbed his back and neck, stopping at his collar. "Wait. There's something here."

Someone had wrapped a piece of paper around the collar. Maverick carefully removed it, unrolling it. "It's from Violet."

M,

R took B. Spy at HWRR. Shipping compound. Get S and trust no one. V

Maverick tensed. "I've got to get to the girls' cabin. Something is wrong."

"I'm coming with you." Buck raced into the living room.

Maverick guessed he was getting a shotgun from his locked cabinet. "Wolf, come." He bounded out of the room, snatching his coat from its hook. He stepped into his boots and flung the back door open.

Icy chills and blowing snow attacked him, but he ignored the cold, throwing on his coat as he headed toward the cabin.

Wolf barreled around him as if he knew exactly where Maverick was going.

Behind him, Buck yelled into his radio.

Maverick stopped and pivoted. "No! You can't say anything."

Buck's jaw dropped. "Why?"

"Because there's a spy on your ranch."

Buck's eyes widened in the dim daylight hour and he pressed the radio button. "Sorry, false alarm. All is good." He stuffed the device into his pocket. "What's going on, Maverick?"

"I need to check on the girls first. Let's go."

The duo followed Wolf, and Maverick knocked before entering. "Coming in."

They entered the tiny rustic cabin.

"Vi. Baylee. Are you here?" Maverick scanned the living space, but it was empty. "You check the bathroom. I'll look in the bedroom."

Maverick hurried to the small room and flicked on the light. Both beds were disheveled, but no sign of either girl. A cracked phone lay discarded on one bed. He picked it up, expecting a locked screen, but he could see a text.

He read the message. "No!"

Wolf pranced around him, barking.

Buck appeared at the entrance. "What is it?"

He held up the phone. "They took the wrong twin and now Violet has left to save her sister. They're both in danger."

"That explains these needles I found in the bathroom garbage can. They must have drugged them both, but didn't care that they left the syringes behind. Sloppy."

"My guess is it was the spy Vi mentioned you have here at the ranch. Ragnovica wouldn't have been so careless."

Buck's eyes narrowed. "I will find out who it is."

"Go get Austin and Izzy. They can help you. Quietly explain to Erica what's going on and ask her to pray and watch Riley."

"What are you going to do?"

"Calling Sara and heading to Asterbine Shipping. I have to save them."

"You care for Violet, don't you?"

"She's a friend, that's all."

"Son, I may be older, but I can still read people. I see the way you both look at each other when the other isn't looking. I know it because that's how I looked at my sweet Becca."

Maverick's final words to Violet entered his mind.

Right now, I can't be near you.

Words he had regretted as soon as they came out of his mouth, but too late to take back. He had planned to tell her this morning that he didn't mean them or blame her, but would he get the chance?

He had to find her and ask for forgiveness.

Lord, please let me find them before it's too late.

"I gotta go. Wolf, come." Maverick stuffed Baylee's phone into his pocket and rushed out of the cabin with Wolf beside him. He circled back to the front of the property as he entered Sara's number.

She answered on the first ring. "Maverick, I was just heading to your place. I have news."

"No time. Meet me at Asterbine Shipping. Ragnovica has Baylee and Violet has gone after her."

A sharp breath sailed through the phone. "On my way."

A plan formed, and Maverick dashed back into the house. He nabbed Violet's plaid scarf off the hook before racing out to his vehicle.

"Wolf, come." Maverick opened the back and Wolf hopped inside.

Time to save both the woman he loved and her twin.

It had taken Violet longer to get to Asterbine Shipping because of the dicey road conditions. Another storm plagued the area just in time for Christmas travel, but right now, her attention was on one thing.

Find her sister and get to safety.

Wherever that was.

Violet parked the Jeep on the side of the road and shimmied in between the partially open barbwire gate. She beelined toward the nearest building and pressed herself flat against the side, hiding from whoever was on the compound grounds. After a few seconds, she peeked around the corner, but the area remained silent. She eased from her position and scanned the property.

The building in front of her had to be the office, but would Ragnovica take Baylee there? Probably not. She checked the opposite direction and noted rows of shipping containers behind a concrete wall.

That would be the obvious choice, but how would she ever find Baylee in the maze of containers? *God, help me!*

Voices sounded to her right, and she ducked behind a crate.

"We put her in one down the first row," a voice said. "Come. Boss lady wants her to get ready for the sale."

Were they her key to finding Baylee?

She stole another glimpse before skulking after the duo through the wall's entrance. They approached a container at the end of the row.

Violet took a step forward. Footsteps sounded behind her, but she was too late in reacting. Something hard came down on her head, and her knees buckled, sending her to the snowy ground.

Flecks of light swirled before the void swallowed her whole.

Violet's pounding head woke her, and she rubbed the goose egg forming. *Stupid, Vi.* She should have been more careful. Now Ragnovica had both twins. Violet shivered from the dampness and scanned the dimmed, tight quarters. She was lying on a steel table but not tied. She guessed she was inside a shipping container. They would probably try to sell her now that she'd breached their premises.

A tear formed and the many memory verses from her childhood entered her mind. She had failed God. Failed her mother with all her bitterness. Failed to protect her sister.

And failed to tell Maverick her true feelings.

God, I'm sorry. Why did I stray away from Your fold? You promised to guard me, but I refused Your protection. I ran away when the going got tough. Please forgive me. If I don't make it out alive, hold Mom and Dad close. Be with my siblings. Remind them how much I love them.

She pictured Maverick spinning Riley and another tear rolled down her cheek. *I'm sorry I couldn't tell Maverick how much I care for him. Riley, too. Help them to grow closer together.*

Save Baylee. Take my life and spare hers. Our family needs her in their lives. It's her turn to be surrounded by the Hoyt love.

She sat up and waited for the spinning to subside. *I give You my life. I love You, Father.*

Moaning sounded across from her.

"Baylee?" Violet shimmied off the table and slowly felt her way over to her sister. "Are you okay?"

"My head hurts. Where are we?" She sat up, but fell back down. "Dizzy."

"Slowly, sis. They drugged us, but took you instead of me. I found the note on your phone. That's how I knew you were here."

Baylee waited for a few seconds before slowly sitting up. "Did you call your cop friend?"

"No, the message said they had spies everywhere. I couldn't risk it, so I left a clue on Wolf. I had to be careful, as someone at the ranch must have drugged us and taken you."

Baylee swung her legs over the edge. "What do they want from us?"

"To make you suffer for betraying them, they plan to sell me to the highest bidder. Let's see if we can get out of here." Violet helped Baylee stand, and they shuffled to the entrance.

Violet pushed on the container steel door, but it wouldn't budge. Not that she was surprised, because why else wouldn't they tie them up? They'd locked them inside.

To wait for their penance.

A chain rattled.

"They're coming," Violet whispered.

Baylee pulled Violet into her arms in a protective hold.

The door creaked open and the first rays of daylight glowed on the woman standing in the entrance.

Violet's jaw dropped. "You!"

How had this woman fooled them all?

TWENTY

Maverick took the exit toward Asterbine Shipping too fast, and his SUV swerved on the snowy roads. *Driving irresponsibly won't get you there faster, Maverick.* He banged the wheel and eased his foot off the gas pedal. *Lord, protect Violet and Baylee. I give them and every aspect of my life back to You, including Riley. I know You answer my prayers, but maybe just not in the way I want. You know best, not me. I realize that now. I'm sorry.*

His cell phone rang over the Bluetooth, and Austin's name showed up on the console. Maverick hit Answer. "Austin, what did you find out?"

"Izzy and Névé figured out who the spy is. It's Gavin."

Maverick drew in a ragged breath. "He's the ranch hand who said he knew Baylee and denied earlier of being involved. Did he say why?"

"Izzy didn't like his answers and pushed him hard. He finally confessed that Ragnovica contacted him via the dark web. Apparently, he had some gambling debts, and he wanted revenge on Baylee as she ignored all his advances."

Maverick whistled. "Wow. And how did Névé help?"

"She found money buried in the snow. Gavin tried to hide it. Izzy called Constable Daley. Constable Everett is on his way here to bring him to the station."

"Good." One mystery solved.

"Are you at Asterbine Shipping yet?"

"Arriving now." Maverick turned right into the business district housing Asterbine, among other places of employment. "I see Buck's vehicle that Violet took." He parked behind the Jeep.

"Mav, be careful and wait for Constable Daley." Concern laced his brother's words.

"She should be here any minute." Maverick put his SUV in Park. "Please pray. We need God's protection."

"You love her, don't you?"

Maverick sighed. "Can't deny it any longer, brother."

"Go get her, then, and tell her. Izzy and I will be on our knees. God's got you."

"Thanks. Please give Erica an update, but make sure Riley doesn't hear."

"Will do. Stay safe. Love you."

"You, too." Maverick ended the call and cut the engine before jumping out of his vehicle. He released Wolf from the back and attached his leash. "Come." He couldn't heed his brother's advice. The twins depended on him.

The two trotted through the open gate and crept in between buildings, keeping out of sight. He noted the multiple rows of shipping containers behind a cement barrier and winced. Not good.

His cell phone buzzed in his pocket. He removed it and swiped the screen. Sara's text telling him she'd arrived and backup was on the way.

He tapped in a message, giving her his current location.

Moments later, she approached with her weapon in a ready position. "Any sign of them?"

Maverick gestured toward the rows of containers behind the wall. "I'm guessing they're probably in one of those, but which one?"

"Good question. Can Wolf help?"

Maverick brought out Violet's scarf. "Let's pray he can get her scent off this. The weather conditions don't help."

Sara tugged on Maverick's arm. "We have to try. I know who Ragnovica is. It's—"

Wolf growled and yanked Maverick forward, barking.

His dog was sensing danger. They had to act fast.

But would they be too late to save Violet and Baylee?

* * *

Violet recoiled at the sight of the woman before them.

Ragnovica.

Reporter Remi Meyer.

"But—but—the police cleared you. You had an alibi." Violet hated the distress in her stuttered words. "How did you fool everyone?"

She sneered and entered the container, her larger-than-life bodyguard following her.

Remi tapped her temple. "I'm resourceful. Money talks. Two years ago, I paid someone handsomely to state I was at that conference the entire day, but after I registered, I snuck out the back entrance. My hacker doctored the video footage, so no one was the wiser." She motioned toward her bodyguard. "This is Bobby. After I left the conference, he and I went to pay the Hancock family a visit. One of Dad's employees told Bobby that Don Hancock was going to testify against him, and I couldn't let that happen. You see, Dad is retiring as the head of Asterbine Shipping, and I'm taking over."

"But why are you a reporter?" Baylee asked.

"It's my cover job. My real name is Amelia Emerson, daughter of Carson Emerson. I will run Asterbine from a distance and my reporter job will help me steer suspicion from my actual business."

Baylee's eyes narrowed. "You disgust me."

Violet stepped toward Remi. "What about your alibi for the attack on us in the park? Did you have your Santa men do all that?"

"Told you. I'm resourceful. Plus, Debb, my cameraperson, is in my pocket, too. She knows that when I disappear, she's always to say I was with her and a source. I like to play the I-can't-reveal-my-source card a lot." She snickered. "Debb's rich father cut her off, and she's accustomed to living the high life, so she needed money."

"Who put the tags in my backpack?" Violet asked.

"You didn't figure that out? Your coworker Jill secretly hated you and wanted money to skip the country to take part in some archeological dig. Didn't take much convincing. She's flying out tonight. Fitting...on Christmas Eve."

Violet's knees buckled at Jill's betrayal. How could she not have seen her hatred? Violet dug her nails into her palms at the idea of being duped again by someone she trusted. Another question rose. "One thing I never figured out. Why cut off the heads? Wasn't shooting the Hancock family enough? And why not bury them together?"

Remi's snickered at Bobby. "That was him. I shot them. He did the rest. Said it was their final punishment for betraying my father."

Baylee marched toward Remi. "You're sick. You help illegal adoption agencies steal newborns. You stole me from my family!"

Remi raised her gun. "Stay back."

Bobby stood in front of Remi, creating a protective barrier.

Violet shoved Baylee behind her. "You leave my sister alone."

"But she has to pay for her interference. Walt confessed everything to me. He's behind bars now, but I will continue his business." She paused. "I had nothing to do with your adoption, Baylee. That was way before my time."

Violet crossed her arms. "But your company is used to transport babies to different homes. How?"

"Mostly through transport trucks. You'd be surprised at the revenue it brings in as well as the human trafficking business. The rings use our shipping company to transport their crops."

"You mean people. They're not plants." Violet couldn't believe the audacity of this woman. "Tell me, why did you bury Amy under that cabin and not with the others?"

The woman's eyes softened, and she chewed on her lower lip.

Wait—she cared for Amy Hancock. "She was special to you, wasn't she?"

"Yes. The day we arrived at their house, the little girl stole my heart. I always wanted a child, but couldn't have any. I decided then to kidnap her and kill the rest of the Hancock family."

The mystery puzzle was falling into place. "But Tanya Ryan, her nanny, got in your way, didn't she?"

"Yes. She rushed me and in the struggle, took my purse before she grabbed Amy and ran out the back door."

"Why would she take your purse?" Baylee asked.

"Because I took Amy's necklace and stuffed it inside. She obviously realized its importance because Amy had cried." Remi's eyes darkened. "Took me a few months, but I finally caught up to Tanya. She paid the price. I retrieved my belongings and kidnapped Amy, but I didn't know Tanya had uploaded information from my tablet that was in my purse to a flash drive until Heather Kane let it slip in an interview that I did with her. By that time, we'd already buried her."

"And that's why you wanted us to find her remains."

"Yes."

"What part did Heather Kane play in all this?" Violet asked.

"Nothing except letting Tanya hide with her for a bit. That's when she told her about the necklace. I had to cast suspicion onto Heather, so I had Bobby steal her van."

Violet tilted her head, studying the woman's emotions. "You kidnapped Amy, but killed her later. Why, when you supposedly cared for her?"

"I didn't." Her eyes softened again as tears formed. "I took her to the cabin to spend Christmas with me. I had hid her in various spots before then, but thought the cabin would be a nice place to go. She rarely spoke to me, so I didn't realize she had a heart condition." Her expression contorted into one of sorrow. "She died in my arms. That's why I buried her there with the necklace she loved and never returned."

Violet almost felt sorry for Remi. Amy's loss had certainly affected her deeply.

Remi cleared her throat, as if ridding herself of Amy's memory. "Okay, enough chitchat. We'll be selling both of you." She chuckled. "Two for the price of one."

"No!" Baylee moved out from behind Violet. "Leave my sister out of this. It's me you want."

"No can do. I don't want you around to spill the beans on my operation. We're selling you both to an overseas buyer."

Violet's pulse raced, sending her heart rate to a dangerous level. She had to keep Remi talking. "But the police have evidence against you now. You won't get away with anything. Give up and surrender."

Remi threw her head back, laughing. "I thought you knew I had spies everywhere. Your dispatcher is on my payroll and stealing that evidence. I'll have it tonight, but you'll be long gone by then. Christmas Eve is a fitting time to sell you as a gift, don't you think?" She turned to her bodyguard. "Get them moving."

He clutched each of their arms and practically lifted them out of the shipping container into the snowy cold. Bobby then removed a Glock from his waistline and stuck the barrel into Violet's back. "Go."

Remi pointed her gun. "To the office."

Barking sounded across the compound. But was that one of their dogs, or had Wolf and Maverick found them?

Maverick let Wolf lead him toward the wall separating them from the containers. "Who is Ragnovica, Sara?"

"We were able to get into Carson Emerson's personal information. He's the owner of the company, and his daughter—Amelia Emerson—changed her name to Remi Meyer."

He gasped. "The reporter? I thought she had an alibi."

"She obviously paid someone to lie for her and evaded the camera at the conference. We checked the footage and didn't see her leave. We also got Walt Dale to talk. Seems Remi is taking over her father's business."

And now Violet and Baylee were in her hands. "We have to

find them." Maverick unhooked Wolf's leash and held Violet's scarf under his nose. The dog sniffed it. "Wolf, seek!"

The dog hurtled toward the cement wall. He stopped and glanced back at them, barking.

"Where does the wall end?" Maverick asked.

Sara pointed. "Down there. We'll go that way."

"Wolf, go!" He signaled toward the end, but the dog remained in place and looked up at the wall.

"What's he doing?"

"He wants to go over the wall."

"How? There's no way he can jump that high. Let me see where the constables are." Sara radioed her team. ETA…two minutes.

"We don't have time. Wolf can do it."

She tilted her head in obvious disbelief.

"He can and will. You just watch what this Belgian Malinois can do." Maverick approached the wall and stood facing it, then bent over so his back could serve as a platform. "Wolf, go!" Maverick thrust his arm upward.

Wolf backed up and bounded toward Maverick at full speed, launching himself onto Maverick's back and up the wall, disappearing over.

Sara's jaw dropped. "He's amazing."

"He is, but we need to run. Now." Maverick ran toward the end with Sara yelling behind him to wait for backup, but he wasn't about to do that with his dog and the love of his life on the other side of the wall.

Sara spoke into her radio, giving the team their new location, and followed.

Maverick darted through the entrance and blasted toward the sound of his dog barking. Then stopped.

Wolf stood in front of Remi and another man, teeth baring in a threatening warning.

Remi turned at their approach and grabbed her bodyguard's arm. "Bobby, take them out!"

Sara pushed Maverick aside, raising her weapon. "Police, stand down!"

"Maverick!" Violet's scream pierced the area.

Bobby fired a shot toward Maverick and Sara.

They leaped to the right, taking cover behind a pile of crates. The bullet zipped by them and slammed into the ground.

Sirens blared outside the compound.

"I have to get closer." Sara eased out from their hiding spot and ran toward a shipping container. She took aim and pulled the trigger.

Bobby ducked, and her bullet sprayed the snow at his feet. He fired again.

Sara jumped away, but failed to get out of the bullet's path. She yelled and clutched her arm, dropping her gun.

Maverick scooped up her Glock. "Stay here. Help is coming."

"Wait, don't—"

Maverick ignored her command and dashed toward the group.

"Bobby, kill them all," Remi said to the man. "They're not worth it. Start with Baylee."

"No!" Violet thrust herself in front of Baylee.

"Wolf, get 'em!" Maverick pointed at Bobby.

Wolf sprang toward the assailant and leaped into the air, knocking him to the ground. The K-9 hopped on top of him and kept his hold on his arm.

Two constables entered the area with their guns raised.

Remi pushed Baylee and Violet around the corner of a shipping container.

"Get this beast off of me," Bobby yelled.

Sara pointed at Bobby. "Constables, detain him."

The duo sprinted toward the bodyguard, pointing their weapons at him. "You're done," one said.

The other brought out his cuffs and restrained him.

Maverick followed Ragnovica. "Remi, it's over. Give it up. You're surrounded."

Remi returned her attention to Maverick. She cocked her

head and sneered. "Awe, the boyfriend has joined the party. How quaint. I'm not going down without a fight." Remi fired a shot.

Pain pierced Maverick's shoulder, and he dropped the gun, falling to his knees.

"No!" Violet staggered toward Maverick.

Baylee rushed the woman, but Remi was too quick. She intercepted Baylee's blow but dropped her gun. Remi shoved Baylee toward the container.

Baylee fell hard, her ankle falling beneath her at a weird angle.

Violet screamed.

Remi hustled toward her discarded gun. "Time to die, Dog Man."

Wolf barked from his position across the yard.

"Violet, get the gun," Baylee yelled.

Violet stopped, eyeing the Glock.

Maverick knew what she was thinking. "Violet, you've got this. You're closer than Wolf. Do it. Now!"

She snatched it and fired at Remi.

Remi clutched her stomach and stumbled to the ground. Wolf reached her and jumped on top, pinning her down.

More constables appeared around the corner, weapons raised. Sara staggered over, clutching her arm. She shouted orders, and soon the team had both Remi and her bodyguard in custody.

Violet dropped to the ground beside Maverick. "You're hurt. We need paramedics."

"I think it's only a graze." Maverick reached up and caressed her face. "Are you okay?"

She hugged him. "I will be. Thank you for saving us."

Wolf trotted over and nestled into them.

"You, too, boy." Violet kissed the dog's forehead.

"Vi, I need to tell you something." Maverick eased himself into a seated position.

Violet placed her fingers on his lips. "When we're back at the ranch. By the Christmas tree."

He smiled. "That's the best idea I've heard all week."

He couldn't wait to share his heart with the woman he loved, on Christmas Eve.

Violet fixated on the Christmas lights illuminating the dimly lit living room. Maverick had received treatment, but thankfully, his wound had proved to be only a graze, and they'd released him by dinner. Frank Hoyt had surprised them all and braved the wintry conditions, arriving at the ranch in time for Buck's famous pasta dish. Tomorrow, he promised them a full turkey dinner for Christmas day. Surgeons had rushed Sara into surgery and extracted the bullet from her arm. She'd be spending the night at the hospital, but had demanded Violet go back to the ranch.

Baylee and their parents were getting acquainted in the dining room while finishing up dessert. Maverick asked Violet to wait by the tree as he tucked the wide-eyed Riley into bed. Maverick's daughter had promised she'd go to sleep so Santa would come quickly.

Watching her parents welcome their long-lost daughter had warmed Violet's heart. Such a Christmas gift, reminding Violet of the greatest gift of all. Baby Jesus born for them. Yes, God is good...all the time. Just like Mama tried to tell Violet.

Now Violet finally believed.

"Penny for your thoughts." Maverick had snuck up behind her in his sock feet.

"I was thinking about all the gifts this year, and I don't mean physical ones. God is good."

"That He is." Maverick took both of her hands. "I need to apologize, as I didn't mean those words I said. I don't blame you for anything that happened the day of Angie's death. Actually, I admire the empathy you had for the shooter and your honor for keeping your promise. Can you forgive me for acting rashly?"

"I did long ago. It's time we both put that tragic event into the past. Angie wouldn't want us rehashing it. She always liked you." Violet bit her lip. "And kept encouraging me to ask you out."

Maverick's brow raised. "She did? Why? We were only friends."

"We were, but she knew about my secret crush. I didn't ask you out because you dated other girls and only thought you liked me as a friend. I didn't want to get my heart broken."

He whistled. "Violet Hoyt, I had a crush on you from the first moment I laid eyes on you. I was just too chicken to ask you out because I didn't think someone as beautiful as you would like me in that way."

"Well, you were wrong, too. I'm sorry we never kept in touch." She hesitated, searching for how to share her heart. "Can you care for someone after what Piper did to you?"

He released her hand and caressed her cheek. "I already do. What about you? I know Jesse scared you away from men. Will you—"

Violet leaned into his personal space. "Shut up and kiss me."

"I was going to ask you out on a date, so I guess that means yes. Merry Christmas, my love." He chuckled, pulling her closer before his lips descended upon hers in a tender kiss.

Violet let out a soft sigh.

Despite all the angst and terror, it remained the best Christmas ever. God had gifted her with another sister, and the man she loved.

The best of both worlds.

EPILOGUE

Christmas Eve, one year later

Violet stared at her reflection alongside that of her twin. "I can't believe how much alike we are." Violet smoothed the white satin bodice of her wedding gown. Even dressed in white, and Baylee in emerald green for Christmas, the girls' likeness matched…to a tee. Baylee had let her hair grow over the past year, and it was now almost the same length as her sister's. While they didn't play too many pranks on their siblings, they couldn't resist the urge to do it once—or twice, making up for lost time.

Baylee wrapped her arms around Violet from behind. "You look beautiful. Maverick is going to swoon when he sees you."

Violet nestled in her sister's hold. "Green suits you perfectly. I'm so glad I chose that color, and you for my maid of honor."

"I hope Hazel, Jayla and Iris weren't upset." Violet's other sisters had had no problem with Violet picking Baylee to be her maid of honor.

"Not at all. They totally understood."

A knock sounded as the door opened, and Erica Hoyt peeked her head inside. "Permission to enter. I know you girls wanted some time alone before the ceremony, but Maverick is getting antsy."

"Of course." Violet retreated from Baylee's hold and eyed her mother dressed in a sparkly red gown. "You're beautiful, Mom."

Erica smiled and took one of each daughter's hands, raising them. "I can't believe this is happening. God gave me another daughter. I'm so proud of both of you."

Violet smiled as her mind retraced the past year. Violet and her mother had a heart-to-heart talk after Christmas. There were tears, laughter, but most of all—forgiveness on both parts. Their relationship was now stronger than ever.

Amelia Emerson—aka Remi Meyers—aka Ragnovica—had survived her injuries and now served time in a federal penitentiary. Her henchmen had turned on her and testified against her, giving the courts a detailed account of the Hancock murders and all other criminal activity. Carson Emerson was also arrested. Police had caught up with Jill Mann on her flight out of the country and she'd been removed from the plane, kicking and screaming. Asterbine Shipping and all the illegal rings were shut down, including Walter Dale Jr.'s adoption business.

After counseling, Riley admitted to her father that she was in the car when her mommy got into an accident. The tragedy had suppressed her memory of that day, but she was now thriving and their father-daughter relationship warmed Violet's heart. Violet had set in motion the plan to adopt Riley legally as her own—with both Riley's and Maverick's blessings. They would soon be one happy family.

Just like the Hoyts.

Baylee had made a decision to change her last name to Hoyt as well as train to be a park warden. Seemed she'd always been interested in their father's vocation and he was delighted with her news.

"Vi, it's time. Time for you to marry your love." Her mother kissed Violet's cheek before adjusting the tiara on Violet's head. She took each daughter's hand again. "Let's do this, girls."

The trio descended the steps of the Hoyt Hideaway Ranch, stopping at the bottom of the stairs, where Frank Hoyt waited.

Her father positioned himself to the right of Violet, her mother to the left. "Everyone is waiting."

Baylee nodded, and the group exited through the front door, following the lit path to the large barn. Light snow fell, adding to the perfect atmosphere for their wedding.

Violet chuckled to herself. It reminded her of the many Christmas movies she'd watched throughout the years—secretly longing for the same perfect ending with the love of her life. And now she had just that.

The group entered the barn, and the guitars began strumming "Silent Night." Appropriate for a Christmas Eve wedding.

They met an excited Riley, beautiful in an ankle-length, green velvet dress and bouncing on her black satin shoes.

Baylee nudged her forward. "Time to go, sweet one. Remember, throw the petals on your way to Daddy."

Riley nodded and walked toward the front, throwing the poinsettia petals on each side perfectly. Baylee followed down the aisle, with rows of family and friends on each side.

Violet caught sight of her soon-to-be husband. He stood proudly in a black tux and green bow tie. Austin was to his right. Izzy sat in the front row, holding their baby girl.

Wolf stood on the other side of Austin. A matching green bow tie was attached to his collar.

Violet dipped her chin at Maverick. Her signal to start.

Maverick wiggled his fingers. A new silent command he'd taught his dog.

Wolf barked.

The crowd laughed.

Violet slowly inched down the aisle with her parents, smiling at each of the Hoyt siblings on her way by. They reached the podium moments later.

"Who gives this woman to marry this man?" the preacher asked.

"Her mother and I." Frank and Erica Hoyt kissed Violet's cheeks from both sides before sitting.

Violet positioned herself beside Maverick. "You look handsome, my prince."

"You're stunning, my love. Wanna get married?" He winked.

She chuckled. "I do. Merry Christmas." She nodded to the pastor.

Violet stole a brief glimpse at her family and friends, then back to the man she loved.

God had given her the perfect gift this Christmas. Not only a renewed relationship back in His fold, but her forever love.

And for that, she was eternally grateful.

Yes, Merry Christmas indeed.

* * * * *

If you liked this story from Darlene L. Turner, check out her previous Love Inspired Suspense books:

Fatal Forensic Investigation
Explosive Christmas Showdown
Alaskan Avalanche Escape
Mountain Abduction Rescue
Buried Grave Secrets
Yukon Wilderness Evidence
K-9 Ranch Protection
Danger in the Wilderness

Available now from Love Inspired Suspense!
Find more great reads at LoveInspired.com

Dear Reader,

Thank you for reading Violet, Maverick and Wolf's story! They certainly had a wild adventure, didn't they? I loved introducing you to Violet and adding in a surprise Hoyt sibling. It was fun to give Maverick and Wolf from *K-9 Ranch Protection* their own book. I also enjoyed creating the fictional park and mountains in Alberta as well as digging into the world of archeology. Anything I embellished for fiction is totally on me.

Violet and Maverick kept secrets from each other while they battled to stay alive. Thankfully, they had each other (and Wolf!) to help overcome the difficulties they faced. In the end, they surrendered their lives to God and grew stronger in their faiths.

I'd love to hear from you. You can contact me through my website www.darleneLturner.com and also sign up for my newsletter to receive exclusive subscriber giveaways. Thanks again for reading my story.

God bless,
Darlene L. Turner